Murder on a Monday

A Rachel Mathews
Murder Mystery

Maureen Grenier

High Tide Publications, Inc.
1000 Bland Point Road
Deltaville, Virginia 23043
www.HighTidePublications.com

Edited by: Narielle Living (NarielleLiving@gmail.com)
Cover by: Firebelliedfrog@gmail.com
Printed in the United States of America
ISBN-13: 978-1945990502

Dedicated With Love
To My Children

Berni, Renée, and Chris

-1-

I opened the side door to our office building, took a step forward, and saw the body on the staircase. What the...? I froze, stupefied, or maybe I took a step back. I don't remember, but whatever I did, Donna, right behind, walked straight into me.

"What's wrong?"

I didn't answer but forced myself to move through the door and up the few steps to reach the woman. She was perfectly still, face down and wearing a fashionable, dark green suit with the skirt hitched high above her knees. Her crumpled body was lying with her head toward the door at the top of the staircase, and when I crouched beside her and lifted her hair, the smell of blood almost made me gag. Bright and red, it pooled out from under her neck, drenching the front of her clothes and spilling over the stairs.

Letting her hair fall, I rose and hurried back down the steps, brushing wordlessly past Donna hovering behind me, unable to trust myself to speak. I pulled open the door, stepped outside, and took four steps before I heaved up my lunch. The only bodies I had ever seen before were suitably clothed and laid out neatly in coffins, hands carefully folded.

The door swung open again and Donna retched a few feet away. I straightened, pulled some tissues from a package in my backpack to wipe my mouth, and handed the rest of them to Donna.

"Rachel, for God's sake, who is it?" Donna's hands were shaking as she took the tissues. "Do we know her?"

"Yes, it's Jody Smythe. She's the manager of Evergreen Manor," I added, although Donna would remember her as well as I did. I tried to pull myself together so I could talk without babbling as I tended to do when upset.

"Is she dead? She must be dead. I saw all the blood when you moved her hair."

"Yes, I think so. Her throat..." My stomach heaved again. "I should have felt for a pulse," I managed. "You call 911 and I'll go back and check."

"Don't touch anything that might have been the weapon," Donna said as she pulled out her cell.

"Don't worry, I won't."

I thought briefly about fingerprints when I reached for the door handle, but reasoned that my prints would be there, and Donna's too, and there was no point in covering it with a tissue. I stepped inside, gritted my teeth, and made my way back up the stairs to where Jody lay. I reached out to touch her wrist, holding my breath as I did so. There was no pulse. She felt cool although that may have been my imagination. I looked carefully around, but saw nothing out of place, nothing that shouldn't be there— except for Jody's lifeless body, of course.

The staircase was narrow with steep wooden stairs, dingy cream paint on the surrounding walls, and a flimsy handrail with rusted bolts that looked as though a good tug would pull it right off the wall.

I slipped back down the stairs and picked up the wooden wedge used to prop open the outer door when needed. The door at the top of the stairs and the one at the bottom leading to the main hall were closed, and when I stepped outside again, I pushed the wedge between the door and the sill. I could hear Donna responding to questions from her cell.

"Yes, Rachel Mathews and Donna O'Hare. We'll wait right here for you. Yes, we'll see that nothing is touched."

She turned to me and looked her question.

"No pulse," I said.

She nodded. "And why do we want to keep the door open?" She gave the doorway a brief, sideways glance.

"If someone comes in from the hall on the first floor or opens the door at the top of the staircase, we can stop them. That was 911?"

"Yes, they're all on the way."

We could hear the sirens as the emergency vehicles approached, and I longed for a cigarette even though I had given up smoking six months ago.

"Bless us all here," Donna sighed. Which I thought was a reasonably appropriate petition.

❀ ❀ ❀ ❀ ❀

Nothing about Monday morning warned us of the nightmare heading our way. I was busy designing ads for our magazine, my friend and business partner, Donna, was out on a sales call, and Cyndi Wanlass, seated in our tiny reception room, was fielding phone calls and smiling brilliantly at anyone who lost his way in the building and accidently wandered into our offices.

I hit the print button and leaned back in my chair, shrugged twice, and rolled my head first in one direction and then the other. After a swig of coffee (yuck, cold), I pulled a creased napkin toward me to proof the scribbled words on it against the ad I had just completed. Donna had offered to re-write it, but I told her not to bother. "We care," I had read aloud when she offered me the crumpled paper napkin, splotched with coffee stains. "Quality is guaranteed." I scanned the rest of it. "It's okay, I can decipher it."

"All of it? Are you sure? I don't want you snarling at me that you had trouble with the ad because of my handwriting," Donna said, grabbing the briefcase she had forgotten to take on her first appointment of the day, apparently in a coffee house. She was smartly dressed in a slimming navy blue jacket over matching slacks and a stark white blouse; her heart-shaped face carefully made up and framed by short, wavy brown hair.

"I never snarl," I replied with dignity as she hurried to the door. "I simply offer strongly worded suggestions because I care and the quality of my work is guaranteed." I raised my voice as the door was closing behind her, "And the napkin is an improvement over the pizza box lid you gave me last week!" However, she was gone, and I went back to work, peace and quiet settling over the office, sunlight streaming through the window.

I enjoy working alone and use that as my reason for coming in later than everyone else and then staying an hour or two after we officially close for the day. No one believes my excuse, of course. I'm a nighthawk and everyone knows that I hate to get up when morning arrives. Fortunately, nobody cares what hours I keep, and couldn't do anything if they did, which is one of the benefits of co-owning a business; however, I've noticed that many people who get up early and arrive at their workplaces before nine o'clock can't stop themselves from sprinkling righteousness and smugness all over the place. They obviously believe all that the nonsense about early birds catching worms and expect to be admired for their potential worm-catching ability.

By noon, when Donna came dancing back through the door, I had produced four great-looking ads for the next issue, and watched, laughing, as she flung her briefcase on her chair and completed her victory dance around the room. I understood exactly what the dance meant.

"Wonderful," I said. "Who and how big?"

"It's a new advertiser with a full page ad," Donna answered finishing off her dance with a flourishing bow. "Not only that, but the advertiser is David, the handsome 'Hottie' I mentioned before. He was charming and friendly, said he remembered hearing me speak last month at the Business Council meeting, and I believe he likes me. How's that for a successful morning?"

"David? You mean David Parker of Evergreen Manor?" I said, shifting my gaze to the window where, in spite of its name, the home for seniors next door was becoming increasingly visible as brilliant gold and red leaves came floating to the ground from the primarily deciduous trees encircling it. The cool fall weather was moving in on us.

"That's the one."

"But how did you manage to sell him a full page? The article on the residence—which you may remember I haven't written—isn't going to be published in the next issue; we've scheduled it for December. Why is he going to run an ad now? Or maybe I should ask, how did you talk him into running an ad in this issue?"

"He's going to run the ad both months," Donna replied, obviously very pleased with herself. "I explained to him that because our lead article in December will be about seniors' residences, there will be lots of ads but, in the November issue, Evergreen Manor's ad will be the only one. I explained that it's our policy to sell ads to accompany articles rather than write articles to accompany ads. Then, I showed him a picture of my wonderful grandparents that I keep on my desk." She held up for inspection a framed photo that I had last seen on a dresser in her guest room. "I said I would have loved for them to live in a beautiful location nearby, if only they hadn't passed on a short time ago."

"Not bad," I said. "Are these are the grandparents you met only a few times and hardly knew? Starting to miss them, are you?"

"Desperately," Donna said looking around her desk. "The only problem is that I have to display this picture in case Mr. Cutie-Pie drops by. I'm meeting him at Evergreen Manor later this week to plan the ad, but you never can be sure. Maybe he'll start longing to see me before then."

"Try the shelf behind you. Be a shame if you lost it under the clutter on your desk," I advised, looking down at the mountain of junk on my own desk and wondering, briefly, how either of us ever managed to find anything in our office. We should do a major cleanup one of these days.

"Good idea," she said, suiting action to words and pausing for a moment to admire the photo in its place of honor before turning and announcing, "I tell you, this guy is single, in his late forties, and perfect for me in every way. Now, let's celebrate my victory with lunch out—I'm starving."

"At The Dungeon?" I asked, naming our usual haunt and pushing back my chair, always game for a celebration especially if food was involved. "We'd better check with Cyndi first. This may be one of her gym days."

"We're fine. I asked Cyndi when I came in if she'd look after things for us and, fortunately, she's not going to the gym today and is eating lunch as we speak: uncooked veggies sprinkled with low fat dressing accompanied by a soothing herbal tea. I have to admire that girl's self-control, but I think she's too thin. She's wasting away."

I didn't bother to respond. I knew Donna would love to pare herself down to some semblance of Cyndi's trim, thin, youthful figure but is hoping she'll stumble on a magic spell to do it. Donna alternates between eating exactly as she pleases and working her way through a seemingly endless number of weight control programs with the results that any sane person would expect.

Donna, age forty-five, is ten years older than Cyndi, hates working out, and claims that her two sons will eat only foods served between hamburger or hot dog buns and accompanied by potatoes fried, baked, broiled, boiled, or mashed and smothered in gravy. We all have our weaknesses, and unless she is on one of her short-lived diets, Donna usually eats what she cooks and loses and gains back the same five pounds every few months in spite of being co-owner of a magazine that includes a department entitled "The Organic Gourmet," which features healthy, low-calorie Westcoast seafood and salad recipes in every issue. Donna is pretty, doesn't need to lose more than five pounds, and looks great in my opinion, but who listens to a best friend about such things?

As we moved through the outer office, Cyndi stopped me, daintily wiping her mouth and hands on a napkin before handing me a photo.

"What's this?" I said, bending over the headshot of a face in heavy shadow against a dark background and then turning it over and reading the note taped on the back. "Drat! I can't use this in the ad; it's horrible." I looked down at Cyndi. "Did anything else come with it?"

Cyndi shook her head. "No, it was all by itself in an envelope. Kevin brought it in on Friday but he came much later than usual and, I'm sorry, I didn't open it until today and forgot to put it with the rest of your mail."

"Who's Kevin?" asked Donna and I in unison.

"He's our regular courier—the one from Hasty Xpress."

"I'll have to call the advertiser about this," I said, sighing as I handed the photo back to Cyndi. "After lunch, of course."

"I'll put it on your desk," Cyndi said with a smile, giving us a cheery little wave and delivering the farewell message, "Take all the time you want for lunch. I'll look after everything." And then before we could get the door closed, she called, "Don't forget to watch the calories."

"Don't forget to watch the calories," Donna mimicked as we started down the back staircase leading to the side of the building facing Evergreen Manor. At the bottom of the stairs, the outside door and the door to the main hall at the right were propped open, either to provide some fresh air to the ground floor offices or because someone was making a delivery.

The main entrance and parking lot were around the corner from this side door, but since The Dungeon was within easy walking distance, we headed toward our usual shortcut to the next street through the unfenced adjoining property. The trees and bushes—lots of evergreens here—screened us from the view of anyone at Evergreen Manor who might object to our trespassing, although objection was highly unlikely since this part of the grounds was left as nature designed it, unlike the manicured area around the residence itself. I had never set foot in The Manor, as I eventually learned to call it, and didn't guess that I would be running in and out of there like a mad woman over the next few days.

I knew the time would probably come—a day in the far, far, distant future, hardly worth thinking about now—when I would be looking at residences like The Manor for myself, assuming I reached the usual age when that was likely to happen. Maybe I'd be lucky and be able to live on my own, healthy up to the end, and keel over in the middle of doing something fun, like dancing the tango.

"I wonder why Mother Parker suddenly agreed to this wild splurge of money on advertising," I said as I followed Donna along the path through the trees to the sidewalk. Birds were singing, insects were humming, and the October sun was warm on my face. Balmy Victoria was living up to its reputation. "You've never been able to interest her before."

Donna shrugged. "I don't know. David looks after the accounting for the residence, and other things as well, even though his mother actually owns the place. Perhaps he talked her into it. In any case, I have his signed contract in my hands and, later this week, we'll work out the ad details." She looked back at me and added, "And I told him where you and I were lunching today—maybe he'll show up. I think he likes me and he really is a Hottie. Did I happen to mention that before?"

"I'm interviewing Katherine Parker on Thursday for the December article," I reminded her. "I'll be talking to David at some point as well. I will, therefore, assess him and report back on my opinion of his 'hottiness' or lack thereof."

"I'm telling you he doesn't lack anything. In fact, he might be the right one for you," Donna said, pausing suddenly and turning right around to look at me. "Wait until you see him. It's about time you found somebody new; it's been a while."

"You saw him first, you can have him," I offered generously as I waved her on, knowing the Hottie was probably a pretty boy with boyish charm to match, like most of the men who caught Donna's attention. We were never attracted to the same males, fortunately, not even in the early years when we were at university together.

"You're so kind," Donna said. "Don't say I didn't offer."

Our favorite restaurant is actually called "The Grand Street Restaurant" but we christened it "The Dungeon" on a dark, wintry day when a waiter with nasal congestion told us about the "turnkey special" instead of the "turkey special," and I suppose the two glasses of wine we consumed before starting to eat might also have had something to do with it. The restaurant is comfortably tucked into what is primarily a residential area, but there is a Town and Country Mall a couple of blocks away and it houses a number of small specialty food stores, a few charming clothing boutiques, a bookstore, and a business supply store. The restaurant is a favorite upscale eating spot that attracts local residents and people from other small businesses scattered throughout the area that don't require storefront exposure and appreciate the inexpensive rents compared to those downtown as we do. Donna and I also love the fact that it's walking distance from our office.

We reached our destination and found the usual noisy, luncheon crowd, but a young waiter cheerfully found a table for two, handed us menus and took our wine order immediately—a glass of Chardonnay for Donna, a Merlot for me. Since we often drink a glass of wine at lunch, we weren't concerned that either of us might end up dozing over our computers in the afternoon. As things turned out, falling asleep in the afternoon became as unlikely as a national advertiser calling and offering to place four full-page ads in our magazine every month for a year, one of our favorite fantasies.

Donna glanced around and then rose slightly to inspect the begonias and trailing ivy that topped the shoulder-high divider separating us from diners on the other half of the room. Her move didn't fool me one bit. She wasn't interested in plants and didn't know a begonia from a petunia; she was checking to see if David happened to drop by for lunch and, after a moment, she lowered herself to her chair with a disappointed sigh.

With my eyes on the menu, I inquired kindly, "No hotties or cutie-pies in sight?"

"No hotties or cutie-pies," she agreed sadly.

We perused our menus in thoughtful silence until our waiter returned with our wine.

I folded my menu and raised my glass. "Let's drink to the full-page, gorgeous-David ad," I smiled.

"To…" Donna began, but I didn't hear the rest. I caught a flash of a "black something" that had dropped to the right of my face. When I focused on it, I was shocked to see a spider had spun down in record speed from the ivy above, and the strand of web attached itself behind my wrist. The villainous creature was now dangling four inches below my arm. Screaming, I leapt to my feet, dropped my glass, and backed into my chair, toppling it to the floor. I desperately looked around for something to knock the spider away from me, but there was nothing I could reach. Still screaming, I began to swing the web against the edge of the table, hoping that the sticky strand would attach itself to the table and I could pull my arm away, but no luck. The web with its dangling passenger swung free with each move.

Suddenly, there was a snap of a white towel as our waiter knocked the spider to the floor and stepped on it. My screaming ceased immediately, and I realized that the room had become deathly quiet. I didn't bother to look around and instead looked up into the young man's face and said calmly, "Thank you. I don't like spiders much."

He smiled and said, "That's all right, you hid it well," and we both laughed. He picked up my chair, mopped the wine with the towel, whisked away my glass, and I resumed my place at the table.

Donna, who sat in stunned silence throughout my performance, said at last, "Well, for goodness sakes, remind me not to introduce you to the pet spider my kids bought the other day."

"As if," I smirked, as though I had forgotten making a complete idiot of myself only moments ago.

"We were thinking of getting one," she said with a smile, "but maybe not." And then, "Seriously, I knew you hated spiders, but I never realized your problem was so extreme. It must be a nightmare; spiders are around us all the time."

"I'm fine if I see the spider first and can stay out of its way," I said, "or I can knock it away or kill it. They don't normally drop on me, and, if they do, I can usually brush them off before I fall apart. However, I couldn't reach anything to brush away that thing on its sticky web." I gave a brief shudder.

"You could have reached the floor."

I looked at Donna blankly. "What?"

"Why didn't you bend down until the spider was on the floor and step on it?"

"I never thought of it," I said, shaken that such an obvious solution hadn't occurred to me at the time, or even after the event. I shook my head in disbelief. "Maybe I should sign myself into a home. I must be some kind of neurotic spider freak."

"I guess it shows what panic can do," Donna said thoughtfully. "Just think—if they only knew how you felt, a few spiders in your apartment could come out of hiding, organize themselves, take you prisoner, and have the run of the place."

Our conversation drifted on to less disturbing topics than spiders, and when a replacement for my wine arrived, we ordered our food. While we ate, we entertained ourselves with a pleasant discussion of the revenue we expected the magazine's November issue to generate and we finally left after paying the bill with the company credit card, including a generous tip for my hero, the waiter. Neither of us were in a hurry to get back to work, and we took our sweet time wandering along the path through the trees, and were discussing an ad that Donna called "The Fat Icky Ad"—an unkind cut at the girth of the advertiser—as I opened the side door of our building, took one step, and stopped in my tracks. There was a woman sprawled across the staircase. What the—

-2-

Donna and I paced inside the yellow taped area that separated the crime scene—of which we were obviously considered a part—from The Onlookers who had apparently followed the sound of sirens to the Ullman Building parking lot. The early afternoon excitement drew a pair of young women pushing baby carriages, drivers who slowed their cars to crane their necks, and people from nearby homes who wandered over, attracted by the noise, the police, and the yellow security tape. I saw Cyndi for a moment in the gathering crowd but when I looked back, she had disappeared.

The main investigator, we realized after a while, was the homicide detective, Inspector Williams, which was a great pity, as he seemed to be the least sympathetic of the lot. He was tall, with a heavy head of dark hair starting to turn gray, and cold blue eyes. He was probably in his early fifties, and we overheard the attractive Constable Bobby Kerr, a much younger officer (too young for us), address him a couple of times as "Mitch." Donna promptly re-christened him—in undertone, of course—as "Bitchy Mitchy," which I hoped he didn't hear, as he didn't appear to be great fans of ours either. Both men wore plain clothes, and a number of uniformed men were at the scene, too. Some of the police had been dispatched to scour the bushes, and we assumed they were looking for the weapon. The ranks of The Onlookers swelled as news of the discovery of Jody's body spread throughout the Ullman Building and the neighborhood, and many eyes were glued on Donna and me, possibly hoping to be the first to call a warning if one or both of us decided to make a break for freedom.

"Rachel Mathews and Donna O'Hare?" Inspector Williams said, turning to us again. He stood unsmiling, notebook in hand, towering over us as though still hoping to intimidate us into admitting that, for some unimaginable reason, we had killed a woman with whom we had only a nodding acquaintance. However, we were ready for him. We had already answered an endless number of questions from a uniformed officer who was one of the first on the scene and who immediately separated us in case one or both of us might reveal our guilt under skillful questioning, assuming we hadn't settled on a good cover story before we called the police. We responded to the same questions when Constable Kerr arrived, and then went through the highlights for the benefit of Inspector Williams; at which point, we were finally declared harmless enough to be allowed to talk to each other again. However, Williams wasn't finished with us, apparently. "Neither of you saw anyone around when you left the building for lunch, nor when you returned?" he asked.

"No," we answered together.

"And you had lunch at The Grand Street Restaurant, you say?" he said, consulting his notebook.

"Yes," Flopsy and Mopsy replied in unison again. We had obviously been through this too many times, separately and together.

The Inspector frowned at us. "I suppose the restaurant was crowded, the waiter was new, and no one will remember you?"

We were prime suspects again?

"Oh, they'll remember us," said Donna.

"You're sure of that?"

"Absolutely," Donna said with what I thought was an unnecessary air of confidence.

"We eat there often, and the waiter knows us," I added quickly before he could ask why Donna was so sure of herself and heard the story that had probably been told and laughed at by far too many people already from my point of view.

"You say this door was closed when you returned from lunch, and you are the one who opened it," he said looking at me. "You are the one who opened it when you went back in to check on Ms. Smythe. And you are also the one who propped it open?"

"Yes." I hoped I didn't sound defensive.

"How long were you in there by yourself when you went back to check her pulse?"

I felt myself flushing. "A minute or two."

"And you didn't touch anything else, and you didn't see a knife, say, or anything like a knife?" He paused meaningfully, as if I hadn't been asked the question at least a half dozen times already.

"No, I didn't. If a weapon were around, I would have seen it unless it was under Jody. And no one came into the stairwell, unless they came while we were losing our lunches outside. That took another two or three minutes." I knew he was just doing his job, but I started to feel uncomfortable with that steady gaze focused on me.

"You have no idea at all why Ms. Smythe would be coming into this building? You didn't usually see her here?"

I shook my head. "We've never seen her here, which doesn't mean she hasn't been here before. Our office is on the second floor"—as if he didn't know by now—"and maybe she has small printing jobs to do for the seniors' residence now and then, flyers or something. Paterson Printing Company is on the first floor, and if she were going there, she would probably use this entrance since it is closer to Evergreen Manor. I don't have any idea why she came here. A couple of real estate people are downstairs, too, and a financial advisor." I shrugged. "There are also vacant offices upstairs. The owner of the building, Karl Ullman, another financial advisor, has a desk and phone in one of them and uses it when he's around, which isn't often."

"And you didn't know her very well?"

"We didn't really know her at all," Donna spoke up, although this fact must already be in his notes somewhere. "We saw her around and knew that she was the manager of Evergreen Manor. We would all exchange hello's and waves when we met."

I nodded my confirmation.

"Okay," he said, and turned away to confer once again with the sea of police officers and medical personnel who had flooded the area over the past half-hour.

"He can't think we had anything to do with this," whispered Donna.

"No, I'm sure he doesn't. However, we found her. We work in this building. We know who Jody is, even if we never said anything more than 'hello' to her. He's hoping we can tell him something useful," I said.

I was still upset by everything that had happened and everything that was going on around us. As well, my back was starting to ache, and I wished I could do some stretches or squats without drawing attention to myself or, better yet, slip into the building and bring out a couple of folding chairs.

"We've told the police everything we know, which isn't much, about ten times. Why won't they let us go back to the office?" Donna hissed, "My feet are starting to hurt in these heels."

I didn't bother to voice my opinion of three-inch spikes in case she took off a shoe and attacked me with it, but I agreed that we were being tortured unnecessarily. We watched uneasily as the ambulance attendants moved from their van to the door and then Inspector Williams glanced back at us and took a step in our direction. "You two may go now," he said, "but we would like you to come down to the station tomorrow morning and make formal statements, and we also need to take your fingerprints to identify them at the scene. It won't take long and we would appreciate it."

"And thanks for your help today." He smiled suddenly and nodded to us both before he turned away.

Donna and I thankfully made our escape before we were forced to witness the pathetic exit of the body bag from the building, and hurried to the front entrance.

As I led the way up the wide staircase to the second floor, I trod heavily on the first and then the second of two squeaky steps that had annoyed us from our first day as tenants in this building and Donna, behind me, did the same. I felt my usual flicker of irritation, unaware that I would soon be grateful that our landlord paid no attention to our repeated requests to have the steps repaired.

The entrance to our offices on the second floor is as unimpressive as the rest of the building with its unmistakable air of warehouse-converted-to-office-space on the slimmest possible budget. A hit-or-miss slather of off-white paint brightened the walls, but the cavernous ceiling was left in its original state, darkened by years of grime to a shade no one would dream of adding to a color chart. The rent for the two offices and tiny powder room that housed our company suited our budget, however, and since we so religiously made a point of visiting our clients to discourage them from coming to our office, we were reasonably satisfied with our quarters. The name of our literary masterpiece, *The Magazine for Island Business*, is lettered on a plaque beside our door, along with the name of the company, MORD Inc. We stepped into the office and found Cyndi waiting with a pot of herbal tea.

"I heard what happened," Cyndi said. "I went outside and saw you two with the police. I decided I'd better come back to the office in case the phone rang. One of the officers came up here to ask me questions, and I guess they're questioning everyone in the building. Isn't this the most awful thing? Poor Jody." She went on, talking non-stop as she passed out filled teacups and accepted our thanks. Even Donna, who normally would have declined to drink what she termed "Cyndi's ghastly excuse for tea," appeared suitably grateful.

"You knew Jody?" I asked, a bit surprised, although I'm not sure why. Cyndi had her own circle of friends, and I didn't know many of them. I felt a sudden surge of sympathy for her at losing someone she knew.

"Yes, well, I've met her a number of times. I go to The Manor to visit a friend of my mother's now and then, and she introduced us. Jody seemed nice and friendly, and is—was—quite pretty. Not very old for someone who worked at a seniors' residence, either. Most of the people there are middle-aged or older. I'd say she was in her mid-thirties. How horrible this is. Isn't it the most awful thing?" she repeated, one hand busily twisting and untwisting the same few strands of hair as she sat down.

Donna hastily excused herself, took her tea into our office, and shut the door behind her, never able to listen to anything Cyndi says without becoming irritated. She rues the day she offered Cyndi the job of salesperson for magazine subscriptions and classified ads, along with data entry and receptionist duties. Donna has the responsibility of bringing in most of the money for our magazine by selling advertising space, and also deals with our accountant, our lawyer, and our banker, and everything related to money matters. I look after ad design and layout, and also write the lead articles, the editorials, and the headlines, and edit all the other articles we publish.

I get along fine with Cyndi, but I'll have to admit that she has an unfortunate habit of making totally inane remarks. She has also shouldered the task of trying to cure Donna and me of all our bad habits with advice of which "look before you leap" would qualify as one of her more profound recommendations.

Cyndi, like Donna, is divorced and doesn't seem to have a man in her life at the moment, but certainly garners a lot of attention from any who happen to catch sight of her long, golden hair and generous smile. This, in spite of the fact that conversation with Cyndi means enduring her annoying ploy of widening her blue, heavily lidded eyes and fluttering her eyelashes at what she deems appropriate intervals. It's an act that ought to lay men out on the floor hooting with laughter but for reasons that are hard to fathom, strikes them dumb with admiration.

Cyndi was dressed today in a powder blue short skirt and wore earrings that were an exact color match. A delicately embroidered white blouse with a scooped neck and short sleeves emphasized her barely faded golden summer tan, but I perched comfortably on the lowest filing cabinet in front of her desk with the confidence of someone sporting new, skinny jeans and a great looking black shirt.

My long hair was pulled up in a clip but I wear it up or down as the spirit moves me, and although I pass myself off as a brunette, I'm not sure of the real color of my hair anymore. Thanks to my hairdresser, it's been many years since I've seen it in its natural state. I'm older than Cyndi, too, and a widow, and since I'm well aware that no one would give me a second glance if Cyndi and I were in the same room unless I were stark naked, I never worry about what I look like on her account.

"So, did Jody and David Parker share the management responsibilities?" I asked, hoping it would help her feel better to talk.

"David Parker isn't a manager. He takes care of the business. You know, the money. He's like an accountant."

"He's the business manager?"

"Yes, that's it; he's the business manager. The managers of the residence are actually Jody and Marianne Levasseur, and Marianne's husband, Guy, helps out as well."

"I know who they are, but I didn't know what jobs they held," I said. "I've never formally met anyone from Evergreen Manor. What do people there call the place, by the way? The Evergreens, Evergreen Manor, or The Manor?"

"They all call it The Manor, I think. That's what Seatie, my mother's friend, calls it anyway. Marianne and Jody run the place, and Guy drives the van for the seniors' appointments and outings and does a lot of the maintenance work."

Cyndi settled back more comfortably in her chair. She was obviously happy to share what she knew about Jody and had stopped fiddling with her hair. The reception office was a calming room, and evidence of Cyndi's organizational skills and decorating touches were all around us. Beautiful plants in gorgeous pots graced the windowsill and the tops of the three cabinets, and ivy trailed from two hanging baskets. Small watercolor paintings brought from her home were attractively arranged on two of the walls and her large desk was carefully polished. Fresh flowers in a glass vase sat beside her computer, along with the phone, desk lamp, in-basket and two open files on which she was apparently working. I thought guiltily of the chaos in the office shared by Donna and me, and tried to sooth myself with another sip of tea.

"Seatie really likes living at The Manor," Cyndi continued, "and she thinks Guy and Marianne and Jody are wonderful. She likes David, too, although the residents don't have that much to do with him. However, he's there a lot and they all know him and like him, I'm sure."

"'Seatie' is an unusual name," I said.

"Her name is Annie Seaton, but everyone calls her Seatie. Even when I was a little girl, I called her Seatie."

"Do all these people you mentioned live in The Manor somewhere?"

"Guy and Marianne have an apartment there and so does—did—Jody. They take turns going on the night shift. If a resident falls or feels sick, or there is some emergency, the person can pull whatever cord is within reach and it will ring in the office during the day, and is switched to ring on the bedside table of whoever is on duty at night. Seatie was really sick one night and pulled the cord, and Jody came, wearing her dressing gown over a nightgown. Seatie will be very upset about Jody. I should go visit her soon."

I made a soothing murmur.

"When Guy and Marianne take their days off, Jody looks after everything, and when she has her days off, Marianne is in charge and Guy helps her. I guess I should have said, 'when she had her days off.' I keep forgetting."

Another soothing murmur.

"Seatie says that the seniors consider the whole residence their home, even though they all have separate suites. They eat together in the dining room and have assigned seats, even though they can make light meals in their apartments if they want to be alone or don't feel well. Of course, if they are really sick, their meals are delivered to them on trays."

"They don't mind being told where they have to sit in the dining room?" I asked, suddenly upset. Is this the fate of elderly people? I had a vision of elderly residents being herded to their places at the table by a prim matron: "Take your seats; no talking; elbows off the table."

Maybe I'd better sign up for the tango lessons right away and buy myself some vitamins to ensure my good health in case I lived to old age, whenever that was.

"They don't mind," Cyndi said. "It's just for dinner. Seatie says the arrangement changes every month, and it helps them get to know everyone. Also, when new people come to live at the residence, Jody and Marianne make sure they are seated by the friendliest and most talkative people so that they will start to feel at home sooner."

I was comforted. I could delay the tango lessons for a while, and I'd never remember to take my vitamins anyway.

"So, they consider themselves well taken care of, then?"

"Oh, yes. It's a really nice home. Seatie has her own furniture in her suite, and it's quite large with big windows. They also have a library with lots of books, and a workshop and a potting room with a—"

"I'll probably be given a grand tour when I go over to do the interviews for the article I'm writing for our December issue," I broke in hastily, more interested in the people than the potting room. "I'll be reporting on the business of running a seniors' residence, and I'm sure I'll be shown around. Tell me more about the people who work there. I know David Parker's mother is the owner. Does she have an apartment there? Does David?"

"No, Katherine Parker lives in a gorgeous home in the Uplands," she said, naming one of the most prestigious areas in Victoria. "I think David has his own apartment downtown, or somewhere. I'm not sure."

I eyed her thoughtfully. "David is quite nice looking. What's he like?" Maybe Cyndi could assure me that David, the Hottie, couldn't possibly have had anything to do with this crime and Donna had nothing to fear by meeting him for a midnight tryst, which might happen if Donna could figure out how to arrange it

"Seatie doesn't know him very well, as I said, but she mentioned that he was nice. She doesn't like Mrs. Parker much."

"Why not?"

"She's a bit snooty, and she isn't very polite to the people who work there. Seatie has heard her kicking up a big fuss over nothing more than once."

"Katherine Parker actually works at The Manor?"

"No, but she usually comes in once a week or so. She's not particularly friendly, but she talks to the residents now and then. Seatie thinks it's so she can find something to complain about to the people who work for her. Seatie never tells her much, she says."

"Who else works there on a regular basis?" Maybe someone who worked at The Manor had a reason to want Jody dead.

"The cook and the kitchen help are there every day, and people come in to wait on the tables. I think they are all university or senior high school students. The cook is the only other one who actually lives in The Manor, and his name is Jake Something. I think it's Purcell."

"What's he like? How old is he?"

"I've never met him. He looks like he's in his late sixties or early seventies, and he's a really good cook according to Seatie. He's quite nice looking for his age and I think she kind of likes him."

I dismissed Jake as a possible love interest for Jody, and thought again about David and Guy. Donna estimated David's age to be late forties and I wondered if Guy were young enough to be in the running as well.

"How old are Guy and Marianne?"

"They must be in their sixties," Cyndi said as the phone rang. "Maybe in their early sixties." She reached up and daintily flicked a few strands of golden hair behind one ear before modulating her voice to reach a couple of octaves lower than her normal speaking voice and breathed a husky "Hello, Magazine for Island Business," into the mouthpiece. Downright impressive.

I realized that I had probably heard the names and estimated ages of all the principals connected with The Manor, and decided I had better leave Cyndi to her work and get on with my own. I caught her eye, smiled and gave her a little wave of thanks before slipping out the door, down the main staircase and into the parking lot to sneak a cigarette, even though I'm no longer a smoker. It's a good thing I carry a couple of cigarettes with me for such emergencies as stumbling across a corpse and becoming a murder suspect. Always think ahead, I say, and Cyndi was likely the one who gave me that bit of useful advice.

-3-

Outside and safely alone beside my car, I gratefully lit up and thought about what I had learned. I knew I couldn't count on the accuracy of Cyndi's assessment of people, but she would have her facts right. David Parker, unfortunately, seemed to be the only possibility as a male who would have interested Jody at The Manor. Donna might have her eye on him, but since she didn't really know him, she could hardly suffer a broken heart if David turned out to be a cold-blooded murderer driven mad by a thwarted love affair or something. On the other hand, it would be a lot more comfortable if the killer were someone else with another motive altogether. Perhaps Jody stood in the way of someone inheriting a million bucks, or maybe she was involved in the drug trade, or she knew where a body was buried. I was glad that I didn't have the job of figuring it all out. The police had resources and would, in due course, come up with the most likely motives and suspects. I hoped Donna waited to see what kind of motive and opportunity David had before she lost her head and invited him out for drinks and dinner or did something equally foolish. Her instincts about men are unbelievably dismal.

I relaxed against my car and stared idly at our plain, square office building stretching two stories above the parking lot, the dull red brick unrelieved by any attempts at decorating or landscaping. I had seen much the same effect created by my five-year-old nephew with his Lego set. The Onlookers had moved on, but police officers were, no doubt, still combing the woods for the weapon unless they had already gotten lucky. From the front of the building, everything appeared normal. I assumed the only reminders of the recent horror would be yellow tape strung across the side door and inside around the staircase, as well, but I didn't plan to go and look.

Inspector Williams and Constable Kerr suddenly appeared around the corner of the building and the two men walked toward a car in the "No Parking" space by the front door. How nice to be able to ignore signs and leave your car in any convenient place.

Williams and Kerr were deep in conversation, but I moved the cigarette to my other hand and pretended to fumble in the backpack slung over my shoulder, just in case. No sense in having them see me with a cigarette and then run into them tomorrow morning when Donna and I were arriving at, or leaving, the police station where we were expected to give sworn statements about today's events. I had assured Donna many times—black-hearted liar that I am—that, yes, of course I was sticking to our agreement to stop smoking, afraid to admit the truth to her in case my treachery weakened her own resolve. It would be my luck to have Kerr or Williams turn out to be a smoker and offer me a cigarette in front of her. What could I say? "Who, me? No thanks, I quit months ago." I'd not only have to worry about being struck by a bolt of lightning, I would destroy the credibility of my sworn statement and might even be moved up on the list of possible murder suspects.

Kerr got behind the wheel of the car, and the Inspector ducked his head and folded his long body into the passenger seat. He looked pretty good when those steely blue eyes weren't focused on me. If he turned in my direction, he'd see me. How long could I pretend to look for something in my backpack? I found my keys and opened the car door. I leaned into the car as though picking up something from the floor until the officer's car had pulled out of the lot. I straightened up, closed and re-locked the car door, and, with a sigh, ground the cigarette stub under my heel. I then quickly sprayed on a bit of cologne from the container I carry in my backpack for such occasions as this. Maintaining a life of deceit is a lot of work.

Back in the office and ready to tackle more of the ads remaining in my file, Donna was on the phone reassuring an advertiser that the body found in our building—a story apparently being reported in news breaks on every local radio station—was not someone from our company. No, no, there is no connection with the magazine at all. Yes, we do know who the victim is, but she was not one of our advertisers nor anyone we were actually acquainted with. No, nothing that happened would interfere with the publication deadline for the November issue. She then repeated everything using slightly different phrasing in response to what must have been the same questions also phrased differently and was starting into it again, when she suddenly said, "Oh, I'm so sorry, my other line is ringing" —she doesn't have another line—and managed to get off the phone.

"God save us all here, that's the third call Cyndi has put through to me. How long do you suppose this will go on?" she asked, her voice dripping with tragedy.

Donna's ancestors are Italian, but her former bitter mimicry of "Tricky Terry," as she calls her Irish ex, has permanently altered the form and content of the expressions she uses. I don't think she even notices anymore.

"I imagine it will go on until you have explained the circumstances to our current advertisers and most of our friends," I said.

"God save us all here," she repeated, and pushed the button to reach the front office. "Hold my calls, Cyndi," she ordered, and then added, "please," as her eyes shifted to mine. "Now maybe we'll have a few minutes to ourselves," she said when she had hung up. "Tell me everything. How well did Cyndi know Jody? Does she know David?"

"Not well and not well." I fixed my eyes firmly on the ad in front of me and wondered in passing why the owner of a furniture company thought using the picture of a lion in his logo was a good idea.

"Thanks. You're a fount of information, you are. It's hard to share an office with someone who never shuts up, and I've been meaning to mention to you how irritating I find it."

"Sorry, but you should have stayed with me and listened to Cyndi; I really have to get these ads finished." I frowned at my oversized screen as I fooled with the font size of the ad in front of me, but dropped the pretense after a few seconds. Donna, who knew I would be dying to spill all, waited until I stopped playing with my computer and told her everything I had learned.

"So, it's unlikely that anyone at Evergreen Manor—The Manor, I guess I should say—had some obvious motive for killing Jody," said Donna when I had finished. "Unless there is a madman over there. Or maybe it's something weird, maybe Jody was involved with someone in killing off residents of The Manor after having them sign over their insurance or their savings or something, and she changed her mind and threatened to go to the authorities."

"Yes, I've watched that story and its variations unfold on TV many times. Let's see—there could have been a conspiracy between Jody and the elegant Katherine Parker and nobody noticed that old folks were dying under mysterious circumstances. Then, suddenly, Jody has an attack of conscience and Katherine realizes that she has to kill her co-conspirator before "all is revealed." Jody was rushing over here to confess to her good friend Cyndi, whom she had met once or twice, and Katherine followed her, drew her trusty knife from her Prada handbag and…um…your turn. I'm out of plot."

"Okay, okay. There are a few flaws, I'll admit."

"I'll say there are a few." I hesitated a minute. "Of course, they are going to try to find out if David Parker was involved with Jody. He is the only one over there besides the university students who is anywhere near her age."

"Mary, Joseph, and all the blessed saints, we're going to find out that they had an affair, she ended it, and he decided to kill her because she broke his heart," said Donna. "He was probably distraught because he thought it would be impossible to find another women, never having caught sight of himself in a mirror in the past forty years."

"I'm sure it was more complicated than that, but you have to admit, based on age, he is the most likely candidate as love-interest for Jody. Anyway, it's very shallow of you to think his looks are the only thing that matters. Being a cold-blooded killer might put some women off."

"You say that only because you haven't seen him yet." Donna got up from her chair and walked over to the window beside my desk—I had won the coin toss for the prized location when we moved in. "But, speaking of age, lots of older men become involved with women much younger than they are, especially men who have money. Think about it," she said nodding toward The Manor. "There must be gentlemen in there who are very well off. Rich, even."

"I think the days of spending money on young women are over for most of the men who live there," I said, thinking about the elderly gentlemen I had seen sitting out in the garden whenever I passed by on sunny days. "They're probably more interested in buying good walkers and making sure that they have the wherewithal to hire personal care attendants when their health deteriorates. Anyway, even if she were unmasked after angling to get named as heir to the estate of a Mr. Moneybags, can you really see any of those old boys tottering over here unseen and sneaking up behind Jody on the stairwell?"

We looked out the window in silence, both overcome for a moment, picturing the little drama.

"Not only that," I added, "if she were the type who was attracted only to money, I doubt if Guy, the handyman, or Jake, the cook, has a strongbox loaded with serious coin; they would have retired by now if they did. That pretty well eliminates anyone Jody would have been interested in and who was capable of killing her other than David."

"You figure David came running over here with a knife to kill her for whatever reason and, lucky for him, no one saw him?" asked Donna.

"I don't figure any such thing," I answered, rolling my eyes heavenward to emphasize the foolishness of her suggestion, although I hadn't entirely discounted the idea myself. "I'm simply saying that if Jody had a love interest in The Manor, the most likely person is David. So, be prepared. But having a love affair, even one that turns sour, doesn't provide most people with a motive for murder or for homicide, meaning she could have been killed on impulse or by accident."

"Right, she might have been killed by someone who impulsively carried a knife and accidentally used it on her."

"Yes, I'd like to hear the story behind that one, too," I admitted. "And by the way, don't forget the drugs that must be all over the place at The Manor. Old people are the biggest users of prescription drugs in our society. Who knows? Maybe Jody stole prescription drugs and sold them to a dealer or a user. Maybe a crazed drug addict killed her. Or it could be something else entirely," I said, warming to my theme of miscellaneous motives and opportunities. "Maybe there is a rich relative in her family, and a cousin or somebody wanted her dead so that he could inherit the money instead of her. The possibilities are endless."

"Yeah, you're right." Donna wandered back to her desk and sat down again. "But why was she killed in our building? Why here?"

"And in the middle of the day, remember?" I responded. "Somebody took an awful chance. Perhaps someone who works in our building killed her. Come to think of it, that's the most likely possibility."

"In that case, I hope it was Ullman himself, the creep," said Donna, cheering up at the thought. Everyone feuded with Karl, but lately Donna was having trouble extending even rudimentary politeness to him. "He was in here last Thursday after you left for your dental appointment. I had to go out into the front office for something and there he was, leering at Cyndi. He switched his attention to me, and I got out of there fast, but not before he invited me to golf with him and check out his great balls. Can you imagine? I was so annoyed, I couldn't even answer him."

"That's just as well," I answered dryly, thinking of some of her previous colorful comments to Karl. "The rent here is all we can afford. We don't want him to raise it because you can't keep a civil tongue in your head."

"I can say anything I want to him. He doesn't notice an insult because he's always too busy dreaming up his next odious remark. I'll bet he's our killer."

"I don't remember seeing his car in the parking lot this morning."

"He could have walked over from his other office," Donna said. "It's only a couple of blocks away. Or maybe the car was here, and you didn't notice. Yes, our Karl went on a murderous rampage this morning. That's what happened."

I ignored this prattle and continued with my inventory of anyone with killer potential in the building. "Old Mr. Paterson is always so busy crooning over his ink supplies and his cameras in the print shop, I can't imagine his caring about anything else enough to kill anyone over it—unless, of course, he found Jody sneaking off with his favorite tube of ink or something. I think Audrey pretty much runs the print shop for him, and those two young women who work there appear to be half asleep most of the time."

"True enough," Donna nodded. "Every time I say 'hello' to Mr. Paterson, he looks wildly startled as though he's never seen me before in his life and isn't sure if he dare respond or not. I don't think he ever deals with the customers himself. Probably wouldn't know Jody if she walked into the shop every week for a year. It's Audrey who takes the orders and talks to the customers, and I would hate to think the survival of my business depended on the likes of Audrey. She doesn't seem to be any too sound herself." Donna shook her head.

"Those two real estate people downstairs aren't likely candidates either," I went on. "That Marcia woman looks after her grandchildren when she isn't showing houses, and the young guy, Mark, works out of the downtown office as well as this one, and so he's not here much either. He has a young family, and I think he coaches minor hockey."

"They also have a young woman answering phones," Donna reminded me.

I dismissed the shy, young mother to whom she was referring with a wave of my hand.

"And their clients come to the Ullman Building, don't forget."

"True," I agreed, "but their clients would use the front door, and there are no windows facing the side of the building in those offices. Even if their company specializes in buying and selling homes for psychopaths and they have killers running in and out of the building all day, Jody couldn't have been seen coming or going by any of their clients. Unless someone was wandering around looking to kill anyone who happened by."

"There are windows at the side," said Donna, brightening up. "Paterson Printing has windows on that side of the building, doesn't it?"

"Yes, and you can see out of them easily by standing on a seven-foot ladder. Those are the darkest rooms in the building."

"Oh, yeah."

"Which leaves only the financial planner, Garth Gibbons."

"No," said Donna decidedly. "He's too fat."

"Too fat?"

"Right. No one that fat could move fast enough to kill anyone. Unless he fell on them first, of course. We're wasting our time. If the killer is someone from this building, it has to be Karl. There's nobody else. Except for one other person, who—now that I think of it—is a great candidate."

"Who's that?"

"Jody may have come into the building carrying some food, since it was lunchtime after all," Donna said—dramatic pause—"and Cyndi got a whiff of it, went berserk, killed her in anorexic haze, and doesn't remember anything about it."

"Do you mind if I leave a little earlier than usual today?" Donna continued. "Going home is the only way I'll be able to avoid more phone calls and answering a million questions. I'm not up to any more of that. Besides, I'm hungry, not surprisingly."

She didn't need to ask my permission, of course; that was guilt talking. She knew the afternoon's activities—or maybe I should say "non-productive activities"—would have put me behind schedule with the ads, and I might have to work later than usual, and, of course, I already work later than Cyndi and Donna and most other people in the building. Donna regularly leaves the office early so that she can get home to make dinner for her boys, but makes up for it by coming in at some ungodly hour of the morning—eight o'clock, I think. Cyndi comes in at nine and I usually wander in around nine-thirty. "Yeah, you might as well run along," I said. "I have to do some more work on these ads, but I won't stay late tonight. I'm hungry myself. But tell Cyndi not to put any phone calls through to me. Tell her to handle them herself; she won't mind."

"Right. She'll probably love it." Donna swept up her handbag, smiled, and departed, leaving me to my ads.

I managed to keep myself so well occupied with formatting styles for the remainder of the afternoon that I was able to push thoughts of Jody's death out of my head; however, I came back to reality with a thud about an hour after Cyndi had poked her head in the door and announced that the workday was over and she was leaving. I was peering at my keyboard and finding it hard to read the numbers, which I was never able to locate with any confidence by touch-typing, when I suddenly realized the office had become unpleasantly dark. I glanced out the window and saw that the evening was fast approaching and here I was, still at the office in a building where someone had been killed—murdered, in fact—that very day. I turned off my computer and grabbed my backpack and jacket. I glanced at my editing file and decided that I had better concentrate on the editing tomorrow before I slipped too far behind with it. I carefully locked the door and tested it before I rather nervously made my way to the main staircase.

When I reached the safety of the outdoors, a couple of other cars were still in the parking lot besides my own, and I identified them as belonging to people in the printing shop. Relieved that I hadn't been alone in the building after all and resolving to be more careful in the future, I quickly unlocked my car door—after checking the floor at the back—and slipped behind the wheel. As I started the drive home, I let my breath out with a long sigh. I was never going to be comfortable working late again, I realized, until the murderer was caught, and I hoped it wouldn't take the police too long to find the culprit. Working late was a way of life to me. Could I ever become a morning person? Not very likely. I sent positive thought waves to Williams and Kerr, wishing them well, tuned the radio to my favorite music station, and tried to concentrate on the road and the colorful late-blooming flowers and golden leaves of autumn decorating my route home.

I thought for a while a car was following me, but it turned off before I reached my apartment building. My nerves were shot, I concluded, and was not surprised.

-4-

I live alone in an apartment close to the downtown area of Victoria, BC, on Vancouver Island. My building has the usual soulless exterior of most apartment buildings, but its saving grace is that it overlooks Beacon Hill Park, one of the beauty spots of the city. My apartment on the third floor affords me a glorious view of the park and a glimpse of the Pacific Ocean beyond, and a quiet street behind protects me and the other residents from most of the irritating sounds of traffic.

I suppose I'll never really recover from losing my husband Don after just a few years of marriage. He died at the scene after a single car accident on the Island Highway and, although I was in the car with him, I suffered only minor injuries and remember nothing of the event, which is probably a good thing. I still miss him, and also miss my sister, who is now grown and gone. Don and I took her in after my parents died, during the second year of our marriage when Mandy was only ten years old. Having practically raised her, it has taken some getting used to living without her, too; however, I'm okay being on my own and not planning to change that arrangement any time soon.

I've lived in this city all my adult life, and have come to accept its temperate climate, like most people who live here, without question. When the dark days of winter draw in and the rainfall increases, we read about, and watch reports of, blizzards and ice storms in other parts of Canada with a faint air of astonishment, as though snow and freezing temperatures occur only in far distant lands. Victoria's location at the southern tip of the island protects us from the extremes of temperature, not the fact that we have somehow won the favor of God, an impression many of us create by smiling smugly whenever visitors describe the less pleasant weather conditions in their hometowns. On the rare occasions that we have a snowfall, the whole town closes up shop, rushes home, and waits for it to melt. It gives the rest of the country a chance to laugh at us; I don't think there's a snowplow to be found in the city.

When I reached home, I parked my car in my assigned spot, not far from the entrance in the building's well-lit parking lot. At the door, I punched in my code to open it, and as I headed toward the elevator, two young men entered it in front of me. They appeared to be in their late twenties, nice looking, clean-shaven, and sporting long, blond hair; both were carrying duffel bags and one was holding a sheaf of papers in his hand as though he were about to make a speech. They grinned in a friendly fashion and held the door, waiting for me, and pushed the button for the top floor. Visitors, I assumed, as I pushed the number for my floor and nodded to the handful of documents. "Oh, good," I said to the young man holding them, "you're going to read us a story on the way up."

He looked a bit surprised and then glanced down at his papers in his hand. After a slight hesitation, he began, "There was a young man named Ned." He paused briefly and then continued, "Who worked hard to keep his family fed."

Pleased with himself, he looked up to see my reaction and I responded with "Hey, that's great," as the elevator came to rest at my floor.

I gave him a brilliant smile as the door slid shut. My storyteller then quickly moved up close to it and shouted so that I could hear him as the elevator moved on, "One night, as Ned was smoking up…"

Still smiling, I unlocked the door to my apartment and headed to the bedroom to shed my office attire and slip thankfully into comfortable sweats. I made my way through the living room to the balcony, pushing "play" on my CD player and grabbing a throw from the sofa as I passed by. The strains of Glenn Gould's Goldberg Variations followed me outside as

I sank into my favorite basket chair, wrapped myself in the warm folds of the blanket and watched the lights blink on, one by one, all over the park, like stars suddenly coming into focus.

Images of Jody's body, the shrieking arrival of the ambulance, the yellow tape fluttering around the edges of the crime scene, Donna's shocked face and Cyndi's wide eyes all scrolled before me like trailers for a film. What had happened on the staircase, and why? Could drugs be involved? The drug trade was the cause of so much violence all over the world and the problem clearly wasn't going to go away anytime soon. However, in our brief encounters with Jody, friend to seniors, waving a cheery greeting to Donna and me, I saw no hint of a possible double life as a shadowy, underworld figure steeped in the drug trade or any other criminal activity.

Of course, I didn't really know anything about the woman and her private affairs, and she could be the head of a drug cartel for all I knew. Who had she come to see in the Ullman Building, and what errand was she on? Did someone follow her? She was lying face down with her head toward the top of the staircase, and so she was probably on her way up the stairs and the killer was behind her. And then, again, maybe not.

Perhaps no one followed her into the building; a person might have been waiting for her at the door and was behind her as she climbed the staircase. Or possibly she had already visited someone in the building and was leaving. That person could have been at the top of the staircase and called to her. Jody might have turned around and waited as the killer came down, pulled out the knife, and... Could anyone slice across a woman's neck with a knife while facing her? Surely not, unless it was in self-defense. Whoever it was would have been sprayed with blood, which would have presented a few problems in trying to get away unnoticed and in trying to clean or dispose of the clothes worn at the time. A forensic doctor would know where the killer was standing, but would the police pass that information on to me if I asked? I tried to picture Inspector Williams confiding in me and failed.

My mind turned to a more immediate problem. Both Donna and I had scheduled meetings in The Manor for this week. Donna was to discuss the new ad with David Parker, and I planned to interview both David and his mother Katherine for the December article. The tactful thing would be to cancel all these arrangements, and I thought briefly about phoning Donna and broaching the subject. No, tomorrow would do. However, we should postpone the article until January or February, in which case, we would have to dream up another lead for the December issue. It would have to be something that would attract ads, but what? Donna would hate giving up her chance of meeting the handsome David face to face again, but what if he were involved in this ugly thing in some way?

I pulled the blanket more closely around me. Did I really want to take the risk of poking around to find out what happened to Jody? If the killer turned out to be a knife-wielding spider, we all know how that would end. Maybe I should just try to satisfy myself that the killer wasn't David now that he had become the focus of Donna's attention and she was, apparently, determined to follow through.

There had been several romantic "interludes" in the five years since Donna's divorce, but so far she hadn't found anyone who was good-looking and charming as well as demonstrating that he was capable of successfully combining the roles of great husband and father. When she complained to me that she was searching for someone with these fairly basic characteristics and it was proving to be exceedingly difficult, I responded with my usual brand of sympathy: "No kidding. And why don't you buy a winning lottery ticket while you're searching for this paragon?"

I shivered and suddenly realized, blanket or not, I was cold, not to mention hungry. Time to go in, warm up, and refuel. I must call my sister after dinner and warn her not to be stressed if she heard the Ullman Building named as the scene of a crime.

I had made and devoured an omelet enhanced with organic mushrooms, green onions, and cheese, as well as a bit of cooked Westcoast crab and spices á la "The Organic Gourmet" and was lingering over my last cup of tea when the phone rang. "Oh, no, Mandy," I thought guiltily. Why hadn't I already called her?

"Rachel." Her familiar voice was pitched an octave higher than usual. "I just heard the story about the woman killed in your building. Were you there at the time? Did you know this Jody Smythe?"

"Yes, I did and, yes, I was there. In fact, Donna and I had the horrible experience of finding her body on the staircase when we returned to the office after lunch."

"Oh, no! What did you do?"

"Fortunately, we both managed to get outside before we threw up all over the crime scene. Then Donna called 911 on her cell while I went inside again to make sure that Jody wasn't still alive. I didn't really check when I first found her; I was too upset."

"But she wasn't."

"No, she wasn't. However, because I went back inside and was alone for a short time with the body, the police really zeroed in on me in case I had smuggled out the murder weapon or something."

"No! Really?"

I laughed without humor. "I don't suppose they actually thought that, but they kept asking if I had seen anything that looked like a knife, and did I really not know the victim, and then they asked me all the same questions over again a number of times. I guess they have to explore every possibility, but it was quite uncomfortable, innocent as the driven snow that I am."

"What a horrible experience. You really didn't know the woman?"

"No, Officer, I didn't."

"Oh, I'm sorry (giggle). But you did say that you knew who she was."

"Which is not the same thing as "knowing" her. We exchanged hello's a few times. I "knew" her name and where she worked but that's all."

"On the radio broadcast, they said that she worked at the seniors' residence next to the Ullman Building."

"True, but I've never been there myself, nor has Donna. Cyndi has," I added, "and apparently she had met Jody but didn't actually "know" her either."

"So, what was this Jody doing in your building?"

"I have no idea. Maybe the police do by now, but we don't. Donna and I have to go to the station tomorrow and make formal statements about finding the body."

"'Finding the body'—I can't believe this is my sister talking. Be sure and keep me posted on what happens. I hate that you are working in a building where a major crime has been committed. You've got to quit staying at the office so late, too. I've never thought that was safe. You should leave when everyone else does."

"Victoria isn't exactly the crime capitol of the world, and there are lights on in the parking lot all night. Anyway, Jody was killed in broad daylight, remember? I was considering doing a night shift from now on so I could avoid being in the building during the day."

"Rachel, that's so freaking lame. You are really annoying at times! I'm trying to tell you that I'm worried about you."

"I know, I'm sorry. I've already decided to stop working late until the killer is caught."

"Good. So, you left with everybody else tonight?"

I hesitated, and Mandy pounced. "You start leaving the office with everyone else!" she practically shouted. "It won't hurt you to wake up earlier so that you can do your job during regular working hours like a normal person. If you have trouble falling asleep at night, take a pill or something. There's medication available for insomniacs in case no one ever told you that before."

"Yeah, yeah, I know," I said, feeling a surge of guilt—not about getting up late or working late but about being such a bitch. "I'm going to reform; I really am."

Mandy was more like my own child rather than my sister because she came to live with my husband and me when she was so young. Our mother had nursed our father through terminal cancer for less than a year and then was rewarded by suffering a brain aneurysm, which dropped her in her tracks soon after his funeral. The arrangement of living together again helped both Mandy and me recover from the shock of losing both parents so suddenly. Don, fortunately, was on board with it, and, in fact, took on the mantle of "big brother/father" quite easily and naturally.

In time, the parent-child role reversal began even though Mandy, twelve years younger, is my sister, not my child. It's that time when a youngster starts to question the parent's actions and also to make judgments and suggestions, often becoming more strict and, in some cases, more demanding than the parent ever was. I was shocked the first time Mandy's arm went out as we were about to cross a street to where our car was parked. She held her arm in front of me until she had checked in both directions for traffic and then lowered her arm and said, "Now" as she began to walk forward. I looked at her in surprise, waiting a minute for her laugh. It had to be a joke—after all, I had been the one to teach her how to cross the road safely. What had changed? How could she possibly think I needed help from her? However, the laugh didn't come, and I realized it was no joke.

She was fifteen at the time. I never asked Don if she had begun to watch over his safety, too. Maybe she did. Certainly, from that day forward, I was increasingly careful about when and how I gave her advice or offered help.

"So, how's our Josh?" I asked, deciding to change the subject. "Is he enjoying kindergarten as much as ever?"

"Yes, he loves it. And, listen, you can see him this weekend, if you like. I need a sitter on Saturday. Can you come up to Nanaimo on Friday and stay for the weekend? I know you hate driving and especially on that highway. If you prefer to travel by bus, I'll meet you and deliver you back to the bus station on Sunday."

"I'd love to spend the weekend with Josh," I replied warmly, "and I'll drive up. I'm getting better at highway driving; I really am."

"Uh huh, sure you are. I'm not kidding about the bus. It will be no problem for me to meet you at the station. You obviously have enough on your mind without the added stress of driving 'Up Island,'" Mandy said, using the term that almost everyone employed to describe any island location north of Victoria.

"No, no, I'll drive. Where are you going that you need a weekend sitter?"

"I have to meet with some people at a couple of different fabric outlets in Vancouver, and I want to catch the earliest ferry from the Island on Saturday morning. I have some big orders to place, and I've already made the ferry reservation. I'll catch the last one home in the evening and so I'll be very late. Elliot would take Josh if he were going to be in town, even though it's not his regular weekend, but unfortunately, he'll be away."

Mandy is an interior decorator and owns a shop in Nanaimo that also sells a variety of odds and ends for the do-it-yourself decorator. Her company is doing really well, and she isn't dependent on the support checks for Josh that come regularly from his father, although she doesn't turn them down either. Mandy inherited the business acumen in our family; I would be lost without a partner like Donna.

"Good for you. That means you have a number of new contracts?"

"I sure do. When can you get here on Friday?"

I weighed the options of leaving work early on Friday afternoon and getting caught in the throng of cars fleeing the city for the weekend, or driving up Vancouver Island in the dark. I not only hate driving; I especially hate driving the highway at night.

"I'll leave work early," I decided quickly. "Expect me for dinner, and let's eat out."

"All right, I'll be home from work by five o'clock, and I'll look for you soon after. If you lose your nerve, give me a call and I'll pick you up at the bus station. There's a bus that arrives from Victoria around five-thirty."

"Okay. Give my love to Josh and tell him I can hardly wait."

"I will. And, Sis…?"

"Yes?"

"Look after yourself. I know how much you love reading your murder mysteries, but what happened today isn't fiction. You should steer clear. I mean that."

"I will," I said lightly, hating the advice but accepting her concern.

"Good. See you Friday night. Love you."

"Love you both," I said, and hung up the phone.

I cleaned up the dishes and changed the discs on my CD player to a variety of New Age music. Forget the radio and TV news broadcasts tonight; I didn't want to listen to a recap of the murder with or without the Ullman Building pictured in the background. I suddenly felt a sharp pang of grief for the young woman who wasn't much older than Mandy and wondered if Jody's mother was alive and if she had heard the news about her daughter. It would be devastating.

I shot a disinterested look at the book I had started reading on the weekend and began wandering aimlessly around the apartment. Normally, my home is a comforting haven for me. The carpet and walls in all rooms are shades of restful green, and I have chosen the furniture carefully, gradually replacing the inexpensive and/or second-hand junk that I had lovingly restored and cared for in the early years of my marriage.

Matching bookcases cover the whole length of the living room wall, home to my collection of spy, adventure, and murder mysteries. Bookcases on the opposite wall are devoted to novels, science fiction, and all the nonfiction books that I have picked up over the years, haunting second-hand bookstores for most of the hardcover volumes.

A long table with six chairs is behind the sofa in the area I've designated as the dining room, and the wall behind the table is covered, floor to ceiling, with oil and watercolor paintings that I've purchased over the years. A modest kitchen, in which I spend very little time, is right around the corner. There are also two bedrooms, one of which is used as an office and doubles as a guestroom.

Tonight, my apartment failed to soothe me. Too restless to look for a movie on TV, assuming I could find something worth watching that I hadn't already seen, I frowned at my large, potted, split-leaf philodendron. The plant had been watered on the weekend, but was now looking limp and neglected. I had been too lavish with the water, I supposed, and I bent down to it and hissed, "I have the power to destroy you. Make up your mind to thrive or you're history."

When I stood up, I decided to go to the top floor and visit my young neighbors. I couldn't get that drug-trade possibility out of my mind, and Mark would be knowledgeable about street drugs. That part of his life was behind him now but he would be able to tell me what I wanted to know. And if he couldn't, his roommate Tommy could. Was David, the Hottie, a drug dealer? Had Jody found out?

Locking my apartment behind me, I took the elevator to the top floor, and knocked on the door to the apartment of my friends. After a brief wait, it was flung open. "Hey, hey, it's the pretty lady from downstairs." Tommy smiled down at me. "Come in and tell us all about the juicy murder in your building." His expression suddenly turned to one of concern. "She wasn't a friend, was she?"

"No, no, I never formally met her," I said reassuringly. I stepped across the threshold and instantly spotted my elevator storyteller and his friend sitting with Mark at the dining room table with glasses of wine in front of them. Mark jumped to his feet and reached for a clean glass on the sideboard.

"Hey, Rachel. Join us for a celebration drink with two old friends who have just arrived in town. They're going to start working for us next week."

Mark and Tommy own a small software company that, from all reports, was doing very well, with sales all across the country. Both men are good looking and neither has that "geek" look that we've come to expect of computer experts: Mark, short with broad shoulders, is built like an athlete, and has dark hair and eyes and a swarthy complexion; Tommy is tall and thin with white-blond straight hair, pale blue eyes, and fine features. However, I don't believe I've seen either one of them wearing anything as conservative as a tie, even when heading to their offices downtown, and their jeans and sweatshirts are a little too informal to be described as "business casual."

"Thank you," I said, seating myself in the chair that Tommy pulled out for me. I took a sip from the glass of wine that was quickly passed to me and smiled around the table. Mark made the introductions, and I learned that the storyteller was Ryan, and his friend was called, for some unfathomable reason, "Hog."

"My last name is H-o-g-g," he spelled out with a smile, when he saw I was trying not to ask.

"Ahh," was my clever response as I struggled to refrain from making any comment, realizing that poor Hogg had probably already heard every possible joke and play on words that his name inspired. "Welcome to Victoria," I quickly went on, "or is it, 'Welcome back'?"

Both young men smiled and shook their heads. "Our first time," volunteered Ryan. "We arrived today and we're going to crash here tonight and start apartment hunting tomorrow, unless the one available in this building turns out to be okay."

"And if Tommy and Mark pay us enough that we can afford it," said Hogg.

Mark grinned comfortably. "You should stay at the YMCA until you prove your worth."

This comment received the derision it deserved, and I then asked and was told that the four had been friends at the University of Toronto, and Ryan and Hogg were also experienced software developers, looking for a change of scene after working in Eastern Canada since their university days.

"Mark and I need a few more contracts before we can think about issuing an IPO—that's an 'initial public offering,'" explained Tommy.

I nodded my understanding. I knew a little about the stock market.

"Mark and I want to free ourselves from our computers for a while so that we can concentrate on some serious marketing efforts at this point. We're hoping these two can take over some of our programming and testing work."

It was easy to identify the interests of these young men by glancing around the room. The effect of the imposing Indian carpet that dominated the living-dining room was diminished by the tangle of cords and cables that spread across it like a giant spider web. These were attached to two computers on opposite sides of the room and several additional screens. The computer monitors were both larger than the screen on the TV, which shared space on a low oak table with extra coils of cable. A couple of other computers and a printer sat on the floor. I wondered what their downtown offices looked like.

"So, you work in the building where a murder took place today?" asked Ryan.

"That's right. And I have come seeking information," I said, with an approving glance around the table at my audience. These people could surely help me. I gave them a quick sketch of the information I had about the murder, and then asked my question, "Can any of you reach back into the memory of your misspent youth and tell me something about street drugs?"

"What do you want to know?" said Mark. Four pairs of eyes watched me intently as I babbled my half-baked theory.

"Yes, some drugs that seniors use would have street value, plus some can be used to manufacture more common street drugs," Tommy informed me, and began to list off some names.

"Wait, wait," I interrupted. "I'll never remember all that. What would seniors be using them for? Maybe that's all I need to understand."

"A lot of older people use painkillers and antidepressants, like Prozac and Zoloft," Mark took up the thread. "And anyone who was stealing and selling the drugs from the seniors' rooms could take only a few at a time or the theft would probably be noticed. How easy would it be for someone to do that in a seniors' residence? Do the police really think the murdered woman was involved in the drug trade?"

"The police have been remiss in sharing their suspicions with me. Donna and I are going to the police station tomorrow morning to make our statements and I am planning to ask if they know where the murderer was standing and what the weapon was. I assume it was a knife, and I assume the murderer was standing behind her, but I haven't heard even those details yet. I think it would be pointless to ask about anything else. They won't tell me."

There was a pause as the men digested my information.

"And I'm simply curious," I added hastily, not wanting to explain that I was interested because my good friend had become attracted to someone who might prove to be a murdering weirdo. "Drug involvement seems like a possibility to me, and I think drugs could be stolen quite easily in a place like that. The managers have keys to every apartment since they have to be able to let themselves in if a resident rings for help and can't get to the door, and, of course, the apartments are empty at mealtimes. If someone doesn't show up for a meal, the managers would know that, too. So, the opportunity to steal from the seniors' apartments is certainly there. And what else would anyone steal from such a place that could supply a motive for murder?"

I hesitated for a minute and then said, "Of course, I'm only guessing. There could have been some other motive altogether."

The five of us batted around a few ideas about murder and motives in general, but no one could think of anything useful to add to the discussion and we all agreed that some aspect of the drug trade could be the answer. I finished off my wine, said my goodbyes, and wished the young men good luck with their new jobs and their apartment hunting. Pausing outside the door that Tommy opened for me, I ducked my head back in and caught Ryan's eye, and recited:

"There was a young man named Ned,

Who worked hard to keep his family fed.

One night when Ned was smoking up,

He dropped his weed in a coffee cup."

I walked away to the sound of his laughter as the door closed. I'd leave him to explain to Mark and Tommy how the mythical Ned had sprung into existence.

I let myself back into my apartment, stressed, restless, and unable to settle down to any useful occupation, or any useless occupation for that matter, and it wasn't time to think about going to bed. I usually call it a day around midnight, and going to bed earlier wouldn't help me fall asleep, as I knew only too well. To haul myself out of the sack to get to the office at some ungodly hour of the morning—like nine o'clock, maybe—meant that I'd have to cope with less sleep and that's all there was to it. The prospect of sleep deprivation added to the problem of nicotine withdrawal, which I had endured for several weeks, suddenly seemed too horrible to contemplate, knowing that the worst was yet to come. I had to stop smoking altogether very, very soon or I'd start adding instead of subtracting one cigarette a day; I knew how this game was played. However, today didn't seem like the best day to cut back to only one cigarette, and so I grabbed a jacket from the closet and headed for the balcony to have a second one. I'd better stay at two cigarettes a day until this crisis is resolved. I believe in living a virtuous life, but there are limits.

-5-

I arrived at work Tuesday morning at a righteous five minutes to nine to find the outer office empty and Donna snarling into the phone in the back room. I was relieved when I realized she was talking to one of her sons and not an advertiser or a subscriber. I quickly opened the bag holding the muffin I had picked up at Tim Horton's and deposited it in front of her. She probably hadn't eaten breakfast, whereas I had wolfed down a piece of toast before I left home. I turned on my computer, took a sip of coffee, and prepared to hear some desperate news after she got off the phone.

Donna finally banged down the receiver and dived at the muffin, nodding her thanks. "Can you believe it? Cyndi called in sick this morning of all mornings," she said between mouthfuls. "I could kill her."

"Yes, I wish she were more dependable," I said. "Let's see. How often has she missed work this year? Oh, yeah, now I remember. Never."

Donna made a face and then sighed. "I know, I know, but people are still phoning to ask questions about what happened yesterday, and I'm getting stuck with all the calls. And then, Patrick woke up with a sore throat, and I had to arrange for him to spend the day with my neighbor since he can't go to school, and he's calling every fifteen minutes to ask me some stupid question. How are we supposed to get to the police station this morning?"

"Why don't we leave and lock the door behind us?" I asked calmly, pleased to discover that sleep deprivation added to the agony of nicotine withdrawal produced a pleasant, zombie-like state that made normal problems seem positively silly. Maybe I could live the rest of my life in this condition.

Donna smiled and popped the last bite of muffin into her mouth. "Good idea. How soon can we get out of here?"

"Let's wait until I've done a little work and you've taken a few more calls. When you start shrieking and cursing and throwing things, I'll know it's time to leave."

"You should have been here ten minutes ago. We'd be on our way. Speaking of which, what are you doing at work so early?"

"It's the new me. I hope you like this. Early to bed and early to rise, and all that."

Donna nodded her understanding, zeroing in on the key point immediately, even though I had carefully omitted it. "Yes, I think it is time you started leaving work earlier. At least until we find out what's going on around here."

"Speaking of what's going on, I think we have to talk about a new article for the December issue," I responded.

"Why?" Donna asked in astonishment, and then she paused and I waited. "Damn, you're right. I guess things will be in an uproar at The Manor for a while. God save us, but nothing ever works out for me."

"Works out for you? Listen, if it's true love, he'll wait," I said dryly.

"Never mind my love life, what about my full page ad for November?"

"Never mind your full page ad for November. What about my lead article for December and all the ads that we could have had to accompany it? It's going to be a bleak Christmas for our employee—no Christmas bonus, no Christmas lunch."

Donna cheered up immediately and launched into a variety of inventive ways to announce the bad news to Cyndi, which left us clutching our sides with tears rolling down our faces: "Will all those people getting a Christmas bonus please step forward? Not so fast, Cyndi," and more and worse. What an awful pair we are. We finally pulled ourselves together and decided that an important matter like the lead article and the ads it must generate should be discussed over lunch, preferably a long one, and we could indulge ourselves after the police station visit. I opened my editing file, Donna turned back to the phone, and we set to work.

The next hour or so went smoothly enough, with Donna managing to remain civil on the phone, and I absorbed in the peculiar punctuation used in the article I was wading through and trying to understand. I came back to earth when someone entered the outer office and I got up to deal with whoever it was since Donna was on the phone as usual.

Audrey Renwick from the Paterson Printing Company downstairs was waiting for me. She is forty-ish, tall and thin with thick, brown hair worn shoulder length, and she owns and wears so many rings, bracelets, and earrings in rotation, she could probably stock her very own dollar store outlet. Aside from her questionable fashion sense, she is quite attractive in spite of rather horsey features, and I find her pleasant and friendly. However, her inability to grasp anything she is told the first time she hears it has earned Donna's ire, and even I'm at a loss to explain how she manages to play a key role in running the print shop. She takes the orders for printing and performs numerous other tasks as one learns to do in a small company, which is especially important when the owner seems totally detached from the customers. Maybe Mr. Paterson is easy to please as long as he doesn't have to deal with people, and if Audrey shields him from that unpleasantness, perhaps any inadequacies in her performance are overlooked.

We greeted each other, and Audrey asked where Cyndi was, but didn't seem very interested in Cyndi's real or imagined illness.

"Our courier hasn't come this morning, and I wanted to ask Cyndi if Hasty Xpress has arrived yet," she explained. "I have a package to go out this morning and it's urgent. I thought I could make some arrangement with your courier." She pushed her hair back from her face with a nervous hand. "We have a customer with a do-or-die deadline, and I'm worried about running out of time."

"Our regular courier is Hasty Xpress, and we use the company only for out-of-town deliveries. We call another courier if we have deliveries within the city," I answered, "and we use several different companies. The Hasty

Xpress pickup for us is in the afternoon, and our deliveries arrive then, too. We haven't phoned another courier today, and so I wouldn't expect anyone other than the Hasty X courier who will come at his usual time. Why don't you phone the company you deal with and ask where your courier is?"

"If he isn't still in the neighborhood, there may not be time for him to get the package from us and get it out in time anyway. Our customer is in Alberta."

"So, get in touch with the company," I said, somewhat impatiently, "and ask. If the courier is late but is on his way, you'll be okay. If he forgot about you and can't get back here in time, tell them to send someone else. You can ask for a 'rush' delivery and shouldn't have to pay the extra for it under the circumstances."

She stood undecided and frowning. "The service we're getting from our courier company isn't very satisfactory. Maybe I should try another one."

I rummaged through the file on Cyndi's desk. "Here's the number for Hasty Xpress," I said, scribbling it on a slip of paper and handing it to her. "If you feel that way, go ahead and try them. We've been happy with our service, and Hasty X is a popular courier. You'll probably be very satisfied."

She stood there for a minute longer staring at the piece of paper in her hand, and finally said, "Thanks, maybe I will."

I quickly asked before she could disappear, "Did you know Jody Smythe?" and then added, "the woman who was killed here yesterday," in case Audrey knew several women named Jody Smythe and wouldn't know which one I was talking about. "Did she ever have printing done for Evergreen Manor or for herself at your company?"

"Oh, yes, she did. We do printing for The Manor fairly often, and we've printed business cards for Jody, too."

"Were you expecting Jody to come to your shop yesterday to discuss a printing job?"

Audrey shrugged. "I don't think so, but I'm not sure."

"Would she normally appear unannounced or would she phone first? Do you know if the police found anything to indicate she was coming to your shop?"

"No one told me anything. She certainly didn't phone, but then, it isn't likely she would unless it was for a reprint order. People don't have to come in if they want us to print something exactly as it was before. They drop by if they want something new. The police asked if she was planning to have some new printing done with us but I didn't know, of course."

She turned to leave and then stopped and turned back. "I guess you heard about David Parker?"

"No, what about him?"

"They took him to the police station early this morning. One of my friends phoned and told me they saw him being taken away by the police."

"What?" I gasped. "Why? Do they have some reason for thinking he killed Jody?"

"I guess they think it's possible," Audrey answered. "I saw him here at noon, you know."

"No, I didn't know. Where did you see him?"

"He was coming into the building by the side entrance, and he was alone. The hall door was open, and I was passing by when he came in, but I don't think he saw me. I told the police, of course. I mean, they asked if I had seen anyone in the building around that time who didn't work here," she added defensively. "What could I say? I saw two people. David Parker was coming in the side entrance when I was on my way to the Ladies' Room. We had the outside door and hall door propped open in the morning because it was so hot and stuffy in our office. Then, just before I started back, a courier came in the front door. I had opened the door to leave the Ladies' Room before remembering that I wanted to take another aspirin for my headache, and I let the door swing shut. I don't know where he went but I don't suppose he saw me either. He was a Hasty Xpress courier.

"And I don't see why Karl couldn't have designed our office to include a restroom like you people have," she continued, frowning and nodding at the open door to our back office that housed a little closet-sized room containing a toilet, a sink, a mirror, and a shelf. "I hate sharing the Ladies' Room, and I hate having to walk down the hall to reach it."

Of course she did. Instead of puzzling over what might have happened here yesterday, Audrey is wondering about restrooms.

I smothered a sigh. "They wouldn't have taken David down to the police station simply because he was in the building. He might have a perfectly reasonable explanation for that."

"I guess you're right, although I don't know why he wouldn't have told them what it was right away. They must have come up with a motive for him or else they are trying to find one."

I stood thinking for a moment and then asked, "Did you see the direction that the courier took? Did it look like he was going upstairs?"

"He was gone by the time I stepped out into the hall again. I don't know where he went."

"Were the hall and side doors still open when you went back to the office?"

Audrey paused for a moment before answering. "The hall door was closed, now that you mention it, and, of course I couldn't see the outside door with the hall door shut."

"And you had no trouble recognizing David when you saw him? You've met him somewhere?"

"Oh, sure. He came over with Jody a couple of months ago to arrange the printing of some new brochures, and he helped her pick out the colors." She smiled. "He's quite nice looking, isn't he?"

Before I could pull myself together to answer that one, Audrey had turned away with, "I've got a delivery crisis on my hands. Got to go, and thanks. I'll catch you later."

She vanished out the door, and I wondered if I should tell Donna the latest news, or wait until she was behind the wheel of the van with my life in her hands. However, I was spared making that decision since, when I turned around, Donna was standing in the doorway and from the look on her face had obviously overheard the exchange.

I said, "You're not shrieking, cursing, and throwing things, but maybe this would be a good time to close down for a bit and get ourselves to the police station."

Donna nodded wordlessly, and we battened down the hatches and set off.

As we pulled out of the parking lot, I offered some comfort. "People are often taken to the station only because the police want to talk to them or to have them make and sign statements. We're going there ourselves."

"'Going' is the operative word," Donna reminded me as she pulled out into the traffic. "We aren't being 'taken,' which suggests something else altogether."

"Maybe so, but perhaps David didn't want to say what he was doing in the building," I answered, shifting slightly so I could remove a child's matchbox car that was digging into me in a particularly uncomfortable spot. "If he wouldn't tell them, they might want to 'take' him to the station so that he would start worrying about rubber hoses and become more cooperative."

Donna snorted. "Wouldn't tell them what? He went into the building to rob some company in broad daylight and he wisely decided to keep it a secret?"

"I was thinking more along the lines of his strolling around The Manor grounds enjoying the October air and suddenly spotting a wildflower in among the trees. He decides that he wants to add it to his hothouse collection. While examining the flower, without warning, he has an agonizing attack of food poisoning because he ate breakfast at his mother's house that morning, and she's a terrible cook. He races to a bathroom in the Ullman Building because it happens to be closer than any bathroom in The Manor. He doesn't want to tell the cops because his mother is right there when he is being questioned and he doesn't want his mother to learn that she had made him sick with her cooking."

"God save us, but you're an idiot," Donna laughed. "My eight-year-old kid could come up with a better story than that."

"Maybe Sean has more talent for fiction than I have," I responded. "What I'm saying is that not everyone wants to tell every little detail of their lives to the police, and David may be concealing something that's perfectly innocent. Or the police may not have believed whatever it was that he told them, and they want to question him about it and check it out. In any case, why would you care so much? Really, Donna, you've only seen him a few times and you've talked to him once. What are you doing? Where are you going with this?"

Donna gave a despairing gesture. "Look at my track record. My first big crush landed me with Tricky Terry for more years than I care to remember. Why did I stay with him for so long hoping to make it work? And who has attracted me since? A bunch of losers. Who attracts me now? Is it some weird, knife-wielding murderer? What kind of freak am I?"

"We don't know for sure it was a knife," I reminded her, ducking part two of the question.

"Right. Axe murderers are a class above," Donna said with a humorless snort.

"I learned another interesting detail from Audrey. When you and I left the building, the two doors at the bottom of the staircase were open. Someone closed them after we left. Maybe it was the murderer."

"It probably was. And?"

"And nothing, I guess."

We pulled into the parking lot at the police station and were directed to the officer who would take our statements. Everything went as smoothly as could be expected, and while Donna was signing her document under the watchful eye of the officer, I posed my question. "Did they find the knife yet?"

He glanced at me briefly. "I don't believe the murder weapon has been found."

I tried again: "Was the murderer standing behind her, do you think?"

"I'm afraid I don't know any details yet," he answered easily. "We have to wait for the autopsy."

Defeated, I rose from my chair when Donna was finished, and we were led to the fingerprinting area. I kept glancing around the station house for Williams and Kerr and was finally rewarded by spotting Inspector Williams some distance away talking to a fellow officer. He glanced in my direction and his eyes met mine. I gave him my most radiant smile, and after a slight hesitation, he returned a slight, unsmiling nod in my direction before turning away. I obviously hadn't impressed him very much yesterday, nor today, either.

"It's time for lunch," I said after consulting my watch as Donna and I left the building. I also remembered my muffin sacrifice and was suddenly aware that I was starving, not being one to face the day with only one piece of toast as sustenance.

"You're right, and let's eat downtown for a change." Donna frowned at an ink smudge on her fingertip that had been overlooked. "I've heard of a good place. Cyndi doesn't like it, which means the food is probably yummy."

We drove a few blocks to the center of town. Even this late in the tourist season, visitors jostled with residents for sidewalk space in front of the pristine storefronts, expensively decorated and newly painted. The restoration of the downtown area had taken place some years ago, but the merchants and building owners were continuing to maintain the fresh, inviting look enhanced by a dazzling array of purple, pink, and yellow flowers mixed with trailing ivy that spilled out of the summer baskets still hanging from the old-fashioned light standards. The scene was vaguely reminiscent of a Hollywood Disney set, and, as usual, I half-expected to see Cinderella or Donald Duck popping out of a doorway. Instead, mostly ordinary people were walking around with their eyes fixed firmly on cell phones and other people were moving carefully around them.

We found a parking spot for the van and headed into the roadhouse restaurant that Donna had in mind. The large room inside was nicely decorated with rich, dark wood, and we were escorted to a comfortable booth with the lunch crowd streaming in behind us. Already seated was a mother trying to eat a BLT in a booth with three young children who were more interested in the crayons and coloring sheets than the food in front of them. They were quiet and well behaved, and the mother, pretty and slim, was sharing fries with the youngest child, a budding artist who was definitely coloring outside the lines, as I could clearly see.

Nearby, two women sitting across from each other were wearing almost identical grey business suits and white blouses, accessorized with black handbags and shoes with moderate heels. My bet was they were lawyers. Both wore their hair short, revealing small, conventional earrings, and they were eating what appeared to be identical salads. I hoped they had something more fun to discuss than briefs and wished I could slip a little vodka into their ice water to liven up their day.

Donna and I ordered drinks and comfort food, which meant a chicken sandwich stuffed with bean sprouts and endive for me and a hamburger and fries for Donna. My ability to let my dieting friend's food choices pass without comment is what makes our friendship such an unblemished gem. "I've thought of a good possibility for the December lead article if we need it," Donna announced as we dug in. "How about interviewing your actuary—the guy you told me about who lives across the hall from you."

"Stuart Vanderdan?" I said, startled. "Yes, he has a consulting business in town somewhere, but how many ads could you build around that? I don't think actuaries are thick upon the ground in Victoria. Most would be located in Vancouver. It's usually insurance companies and big organizations with pension and health plans that require services of an actuary, and most businesses on the Island are too small, or their head offices are elsewhere. Stuart works here because he wants to be close to his daughter and his grandchildren, and I don't think he cares how much money he makes. He might be the only working actuary in town."

"I thought you told me that actuaries are rivals of accountants, and they're always making jokes about each other."

"Yes: what's the difference between an actuary and an accountant? The actuary has a personality," I responded on cue. "The fact is, they do different work but use each other's numbers, and they actually work quite cooperatively, I believe. Stuart told me that an accountant's version of the joke is, what's the difference between an actuary and an accountant? The *accountant* has a personality."

"There you go, then. We could get ads from accounting firms in town."

I frowned. "How? I just said that accountants don't do the same job. Why would they care if we have a lead article about actuaries?"

"You said they work cooperatively, didn't you? They both deal in numbers, don't they? They do year-end work, right? Get Stuart to talk about what he does with businesses and make sure he talks about the accountants. You can do it."

I stared at her in exasperation. "So, I tell Stuart that I want to interview him about his consulting work and the role of actuaries in business, but the main thing I want to know about is the accountant's job. He'll love it. He'll talk for hours. I won't be able to shut him up. Why don't we do an article about accountants?"

"Holy Saints in Heaven, Rachel, show a little imagination. We just did an article about accountants five months ago. We can't do another one so soon."

"Have you considered that Stuart might want to know why I'm not interviewing an accountant?" I pointed out. "What do I say to that?"

"He's a friend, isn't he? Why don't you tell him the truth?"

"The truth? Hey, that's a wild idea," I replied, trying not to sneer and expose the chicken bits caught between my teeth. "Why don't we pull the January lead into December instead? What do we have planned for January? I've forgotten."

"We are going to do the financial advisor thingy. January is when the financial advisors will want to advertise, not December."

"So much for our policy of selling ads around our articles rather than writing articles around our ads," I said peevishly.

"Ah, who believes that one anyway?" Donna laughed. "I say it and the advertisers pretend to believe me. It's a game. And I'm not kidding about the article. I'm sure I could sell advertising around it. Tell Stuart that you think the world should know the difference between an accountant and an actuary, and you need to generate some ads from the accountants. If he doesn't care about money and accountants aren't rivals, why would he mind? Come on, Rachel, show some spirit. I don't mind Cyndi doing without a Christmas bonus, but I want mine."

I took a sip of wine and thought it over. Stuart was so shy and pleasant, he probably wouldn't refuse no matter what he privately thought. I tried to imagine an approach I could take. Finally, I said, "Okay, you win. I'll take a shot at it," and sighed. "He's such a nice guy, I hate to take advantage of him."

"What advantage? He gets some free publicity with hardly any effort at all. You can interview him at your place. Invite him over for coffee. Tell him we'll run a two-by four-inch ad with his company name and address and phone number in addition to the article. That'll fetch him."

"Tell you what," I said, brightening up. "When I arrange this interview, you drop by and I'll introduce you. He told me that his wife died a few years ago. Maybe you'll look into each other's eyes and realize you were meant to be together. It could be the start of a great relationship for the two of you."

"You've been trying to set me up with this neighbor of yours for the last six months. Forget it. If he's as shy and introverted as you've described, what's he going to think of my Patrick and Sean squabbling and tearing my house apart? One look at them and he'd flee into the night never to be seen again. Besides, what's wrong with him? How old is he? Why haven't you gone out on a date with him?"

"He's never asked me. He's quite nice looking and in his early fifties, I would say. I don't think he dates anyone. He's shy, remember? He probably asked his wife for a date in a hormonal burst of sociability when he was at university, and that was the end of it. She likely took over from there."

"So, why would he suddenly ask me out?"

"I doubt if he will, but I thought maybe you would do the asking; you're not shy. You could rescue the poor guy."

"Why don't you rescue him? I'll bet he's been pining for you ever since he moved into the building."

"Because I'm shy, too, and we've already established ourselves as friends only—there's no spark between us. He's more your type, and I think you'd like him," I said, not bothering to point out that whatever his shortcomings, at least he wasn't a suspect in a murder case.

"Let's get the article out of the way first, then I'll think about a rescue job." We smiled at each other amicably.

The rest of the day was unremarkable and the evening dragged. I spent most of it on household chores and part of it on my balcony huddled in a jacket, smoking my allotment of two cigarettes and wondering how to approach Stuart. He had certainly responded to me when I smiled and spoke to him on those rare occasions when we ran into each other, and I had thought once or twice about inviting him over for a cup of coffee just to be neighborly, but knew if he interpreted it as a demented neighbor putting the moves on him, he might start going out of his way to avoid me. No sense in stressing out the poor man. He had answered my questions about actuaries when I asked, and he seemed to enjoy telling me the latest actuarial jokes. The last one was, how can you tell an extroverted actuary from an introverted actuary? Apparently, an introverted actuary stares at his shoes when he is talking to you, and an extroverted actuary stares at *your* shoes when he's talking to you. Well, Stuart wasn't that bad. He could carry on a conversation when a topic was introduced, and he obviously had a good sense of humor. He might enjoy talking about his work, and maybe I could work a couple of his actuarial jokes into the article I wrote. I finally decided to prepare a series of questions to ask him and try my luck later in the week. Before Friday night, of course, since I was going to Nanaimo to spend some time with Josh.

I forced myself to go to bed early, but couldn't get to sleep in spite of my valiant effort to prepare myself by drinking a cup of warm milk while taking a pleasant soak in a lavender-oil perfumed bath, knocking back 100 milligrams of Vitamin B, the stress-relieving vitamin, and then forcing myself to read a full chapter of *Canada, A Story of Challenge*, guaranteed to put an entire class of freshmen to sleep at ten o'clock in the morning. Nothing helped. An hour later, I was still tossing from side to side, wondering what more I could do when I suddenly remembered that taking aspirin could help, at least in the short-term, and so I got out of bed and chugged back a couple of them with a glass of water. Where would this all end, I wondered grimly as I crawled back into bed. My last conscious thought was to hope that Inspector Williams was having as much trouble sleeping as I was and would redouble his efforts to solve our mystery.

-6-

The next day, I dragged myself to work at the appointed hour and was startled to find two police cars, as well as an unidentified car in the No Parking zone, which suggested Williams and Kerr were here, too. "Now what?" I asked myself, alarm bells clanging in my head as I hurried up the stairs. The sight that greeted me was a very crowded office with police swarming everywhere. I soon narrowed that down to Inspector Williams and Constable Kerr questioning a bewildered-looking Cyndi, and a uniformed officer taking notes. Another uniformed policeman was just turning away from Donna who was literally wringing her hands. I had never seen her do that before.

"What happened?" I asked, moving toward her, dodging a police officer to do so.

"They've found Kevin, our courier. He's dead, and they think there is some connection between his death and Jody's," Donna said in an undertone. "And David has been released. I guess his lawyer looked after things, and they let him go home last night."

"How did Kevin die?" I asked, horrified, and not interested at the moment in David's fate.

Inspector Williams was suddenly right there beside me. "Someone cut his throat," he answered grimly. "When did you see him last?"

If he was trying to shock me, it worked. "It was one afternoon last week," I said, feeling a little dizzy as I turned to face him. "I'm not sure of the day—Tuesday or Wednesday, I think. Kevin or someone else from Hasty X comes roughly around three-thirty in the afternoon to deliver anything sent to us and to pick up anything we have going out. It's a scheduled time for our out-of-town deliveries. Cyndi mentioned that she saw Kevin on Friday."

"Did he come here this past Monday?"

"He didn't come yesterday, Tuesday," I said, pausing to think. "It was some other courier. Cyndi would know if Kevin came Monday or not, but I don't."

"Cyndi told us the last time she saw him was Friday. So, you're saying that you wouldn't ever expect him to come here in the morning—only in the afternoon?"

"We wouldn't expect him to come to *our* office, but he could be here picking up or delivering for someone else in the building. I think he would try to make all trips to the same building at the same time of day, but maybe he can't always arrange that. I'm not sure. Audrey Renwick, the woman who works in the print shop downstairs, saw a Hasty X courier coming in the front door around noon on Monday."

"She told you it was someone from Hasty Xpress?"

"Yes," I answered.

"She told us that she wasn't sure if it was someone from Hasty Xpress or from another courier company, and then said she didn't really get a good look at him. We'll have to talk to her again."

"She definitely mentioned Hasty Xpress when she spoke to me," I said. "Where and when was Kevin found?"

"In a treed area behind the Hasty X Building last night. A man who was walking his dog late in the evening phoned to tell us his dog had led him to a body in the brush. The dog wasn't on a leash, and because he barked and howled and wouldn't come when his owner called him, the guy investigated. We think Mr. Lewis might have been killed within hours of Jody—before or after. We won't know for sure until the autopsy is performed."

"Had no one reported him missing?" I asked, appalled, but reminding myself that the Hasty X building was a few miles away.

"Oh, yes. His company reported to the police that both the courier and his van were missing at the end of the day on Monday, and his wife was notified, too. She filed a missing persons report as soon as we could accept one, which was Tuesday afternoon.

"The van was found Monday evening, locked, with the keys inside. We've been told that nothing is missing as far as the company knows, except for the clipboard and sheets that the customers sign when a delivery is made. They don't think any deliveries were made that day and are still checking on that. A lot of letters and packages were inside the van, and it was parked at the Town and Country Mall. Mr. Lewis, of course, wasn't found until last night, Tuesday night."

I worked out that "Kevin" must be "Mr. Lewis." The aforementioned mall was three short blocks away, a fact that would not go unremarked by the police. "How could it take the company all day to realize he was missing?" I asked. "Didn't anyone from his office try to contact him earlier?"

"He picked up his deliveries and prepared the customer sign-off sheets on Monday morning at the Hasty Xpress Building as usual," the Inspector answered, lowering his voice so that only Donna and I could hear. By sharing information with us, he was, no doubt, hoping to gain our confidence so that we would tell him whatever we knew. A pity, since neither of us had any useful information about our young courier.

"Lewis would normally download the information about what he picks up on a mini-computer in his van during the day and the information would automatically be recorded on a computer at the office," he went on. "When the information comes in regularly, the dispatcher knows where the courier is on his route, but when the couriers become busy, they often delay processing a lot of this information until the end of the day when they return to the office. When Mr. Lewis didn't show up at various locations to make his pickups, customers began calling the office to complain. The dispatcher tried to phone Mr. Lewis on his cell phone, but there was no response. Again, that's not too surprising since the couriers often can't receive calls when they are in large office buildings, in elevators, and so on. Eventually, the dispatcher called other drivers to cover Mr. Lewis's territory, and assumed he had become ill or had had an accident and was tied up with that. The dispatcher expected to hear from him sooner or later, which, of course, didn't happen. So, we were notified.

"How well were you people acquainted with him?" Inspector Williams added, pen poised over his notebook.

Donna and I looked at each other and she shook her head. "I guess only Cyndi really knew him," I said, looking over to where Cyndi was still occupied with Constable Kerr and a uniformed officer, "but they weren't exactly friends. She mentioned his name for the first time on Monday."

"He's quite young," Donna said by way of explanation, implying that he was too young to interest Cyndi.

"He was old enough to be married and have two little girls," Williams replied, scribbling in his notepad. "Did he usually wear a cap? A Hasty X cap?"

"Oh, God," I said, blinking through a sting of tears, not able to think for a moment of anything but the tragedy for the young family.

Williams repeated the question, and I pulled myself together and looked at Donna doubtfully. "I think so," I said drawing a deep breath, "but Cyndi would know that better than we would. She's the one who usually deals with the couriers."

Williams nodded and snapped his notebook shut. "She thinks he usually wore one and, in that case, his cap seems to be missing, as well as his clipboard." He reached into his pocket and handed his business cards to everyone before he and the others headed to the door. "Call if you remember anything that might help us."

I followed the Inspector after glancing down at his card and noting again that his first name was 'Mitch,' and stood watching as the officers started down the stairs. Williams paused and looked at the name plaque beside our door. "What does MORD mean?" he asked, nodding towards the plaque and our company name in small print under the name of the magazine.

"It's the result of taking the lazy way out when naming a company," I said, a little stiffly, hoping he hadn't added the "Inc" when he said the name to himself. I was really tired of explaining how that had happened. "'M' stands for Mathews, 'O' for O'Hare, 'R' for Rachel, and 'D' for Donna."

Mitch nodded without smiling, which pleased me, and he continued on his way down the stairs. Perhaps he was good at maintaining a poker face no matter what thought wandered into his head. Cops have to be good at that, I guess.

Cyndi was listening to recorded messages on the answering machine and making notes as I passed by her desk. She looked up and gave me a pathetic little smile. Her face was pale, but, aside from that, she looked well enough. Donna was checking her appointment book and waited until I was settled behind my desk and had taken a sip of the coffee I had brought to the office with me and had been clutching ever since. It was cold, of course, and I made a face as I put it down.

"So, what do you think?" she asked. "Was Kevin's murder related to Jody's?"

"Had to be, I suppose. 'I can't believe six impossible things before breakfast,'" I quoted. "His cap and his clipboard are missing. So, the murderer wore the cap and carried the clipboard into the building, hoping it would be some kind of disguise, and Audrey saw him."

"Except she's not sure now that he really was from Hasty X, which means she didn't notice the name on the cap."

"Audrey's a nice woman but, as you know, a bubble-head," I said impatiently. "She's never sure about anything, and I'd be inclined to go with her first impression. She told me that the man was a Hasty Xpress courier. She probably recognized the Hasty Xpress cap on someone, and now she's had second thoughts about it only because it's important. If something matters, she automatically becomes indecisive and I hope the police jump all over her for it. She can probably identify whoever it was. I can't bear to think of those little girls losing their father, and in such a terrible, senseless way."

"Surely you don't suppose Kevin was murdered because someone wanted his cap."

"I don't know why he was murdered, but if a Hasty Xpress cap appeared here on somebody's head around the time that Jody was murdered, and Kevin's cap has disappeared, it certainly looks suspicious."

Donna nodded slowly and gazed down at her appointment book. "Well, I'm glad they released David," she said. "They mustn't have found any reason that he would want to kill Jody or else they checked on his alibi and were satisfied that he couldn't have done it."

"I suppose so."

"Which means that I can now call him and confirm the appointment to discuss his ad."

"Wait a minute. I'm not sure we should go ahead with that. And didn't you talk me into doing an interview with my actuary for the December issue at lunch yesterday? David probably won't want to advertise if we aren't doing the story about The Manor in December, and how can we? David and his mother have probably gone through so many interviews with the police by now, they'll probably scream at anyone who asks them their names, never mind being willing to answer questions about the business case for running a seniors' residence."

"I'm not so sure about that," Donna remarked dreamily, obviously forgetting that the object of her attention might be a crazed, knife-wielding killer who had managed to temporarily fool the cops into believing that he was busy elsewhere at the time of two murders. I felt like opening my mouth and letting out a great bellow of rage and then decided that with nothing to go on other than my usual doubt and suspicion about everything and everyone, I should control myself.

"Are you going to call and ask him about the ad then?" I asked.

"Sure, why not?"

Why not, indeed? "Well, you tell him that we are certainly able to run another article in December so that we don't have to bother them with an interview at this difficult time."

"At this difficult time?" Donna said. "Is that a line out of a sympathy card?"

"Probably, and may I point out that it's very appropriate at this difficult time."

"Well, okay," she said, heaving a great self-pitying sigh as though I had suddenly insisted that she submit all her ad material to me in Sanskrit. "You're probably right. I'll ask David for an appointment about the ad and ask him how he and his mother would feel about going ahead with the interviews for the article. I'll warn him that we are preparing another article just in case."

"Good." Satisfied with small mercies, I opened my computer and set to work, trying not to think of Kevin's little family. I also engaged my talent for turning off background noise so that I wouldn't have to listen to how Donna handled her sales pitch "at this difficult time."

"Rachel," Donna said urgently, summoning me from the depths of an article on insurance needs for small businesses. She motioned to my phone, and I reached for it as she quickly brought me up to speed. "David is on line two. He is going to run the ad this month and will talk to you about the interviews."

I picked up the phone and fixed a smile on my face. "Hi, there. Has Donna explained that we were a bit worried about bothering you with an interview right now? We don't want to intrude, and we can do the article later when it is more convenient for you."

I listened while David assured me that he would consult his mother for her views on the subject. He didn't mind at all, but his mother, of course, might wish to delay things, and he was glad we understood. He added that she was helping out at the office in this crisis, but she had gone home for the day. This whole thing was very upsetting to her. He knew we were counting on them and didn't want to let us down, but naturally...

I mouthed all the proper consoling remarks, and we left it at his promising to get in touch with me after he had talked to his mother. He really did sound very nice with his warm, deep voice saying all the right things, and I sighed as I hung up the phone. Donna, with her crush on him, was probably a dead duck if he was as pleasant in person as he looked and sounded. I decided not to pursue that unfortunate choice of metaphor.

I forced myself to smile as she sat waiting expectantly. "He'll be in touch about the article after he consults Katherine."

"See?" said Donna triumphantly. "He's very pleased about placing an ad this month whether or not an article is published soon because he wants to diffuse any bad publicity Jody's murder might have created. I guessed he wouldn't mind doing an interview for an article for the same reason. Of course, we don't know what Katherine will decide, and so you had better go ahead and interview your actuary to be on the safe side, but I'm betting we will get the go-ahead from her as well. I've heard she's a shrewd business person. I'm going to be able to keep the appointment to see David on Friday and will help him work out an appropriate ad that can be used for both November and December just by changing the illustration."

"Gotcha," I said returning to my insurance article, noting with awe that the author had somehow managed to start every single sentence with a subordinate clause.

The rest of the day passed uneventfully, and Donna left at her usual time, not nearly as upset about the second murder on Monday as I thought she should be. At five o'clock, Cyndi came in to see me.

"Gosh, Rachel, I can't decide what to do," she said, and I sat waiting for some horrible revelation. "I exchanged a blouse for Seatie, and I have the new one for her at home, but I can't bear to go over to The Manor this week. I still don't feel well, and I don't want to go and have a long talk with her about everything. I really like her, but ..." and she looked at me expectantly.

Was that all? Well, here was my chance to get first-hand info on David from a possibly observant (read "nosey") old dear who was right on the spot. I could also tactfully ask about items (read "drugs") that might be disappearing from the seniors' apartments. Good stuff.

"Why I'd be happy to take it over to your friend if you like," I said with a big smile to show my enthusiasm. "Bring the blouse to me and I'll pop over with it. I don't mind at all."

"Gee, thanks, Rachel, that would be great. I'll bring it tomorrow in case she wants it for the weekend. Will that be all right? Can you take it over to her tomorrow?" Her relief was very apparent. Maybe she really was still under the weather.

"No problem. Tomorrow it is." We exchanged smiles and, as soon as Cyndi left, I turned off my computer and departed.

When I reached the parking lot, I saw Audrey and hailed her as she was getting into her car. "How did it go?" I asked, hurrying over to her.

"Oh, everything was fine, thanks. The courier company sent someone to pick up the envelope right away and our customer called this morning to tell us he was pleased with the printing job."

I stared, puzzled, and then understood. "No, no, I wasn't talking about your courier problem; I meant, how was your interview with the police?"

"The police?"

"Didn't they come by and ask you again about the Hasty Xpress courier you saw on Monday?" I asked, stifling an urge to reach over and shake her in hopes of waking her up.

"Oh, that. Well, I told them I'm not sure the courier was from Hasty Xpress. I didn't really look at him—it was only a glance."

"You told me that he was from Hasty X."

"Maybe he was," she said with a shrug. "I'm not sure anymore."

"He was wearing a courier's cap, wasn't he?" I persisted, wondering how she managed to drive a car and shop for groceries all by herself.

"I think so."

"Did the police show you a picture of Kevin?"

"Yes, but I don't know if it was him or not. I'm not sure. I've got to run, Rachel. Sorry." She got into the car, gave me a little wave, and I stood watching our star witness literally drive off into the sunset. The only thing missing was a big "The End" plastered across the scene.

That night, as I drifted in and out of a restless sleep, I struggled desperately to forget the fate of two people whose lives had touched mine, no matter how briefly. At two o'clock, I gave up, turned on my bedside lamp and began reading the second chapter of *Canada, A Story of Challenge*. I'm pleased to report that after reading the happy news that John Cabot had discovered the great fishing banks off the coast of North America, I finally blanked out. Way to go, John.

-7-

Cyndi was late coming into the office on Thursday morning—something I wouldn't have known in the good old days when I wandered into the office at my usual civilized hour—but she was carrying her excuse in her hand when she arrived. It was a large, variegated green plant in an attractive ceramic pot, which looked brand new. We had left the door open between our offices in order to tend to any receptionist duties her lateness created for us, and so we were able to watch as she set the plant down on her desk, smile cheerily at us, and then disappear again.

"She must have run out of counter and desk space for plants," remarked Donna. "I see a great length of chain she is going to use to suspend this new one from the ceiling, unless, of course, she is planning to drape that chain around her hips. Did you notice if she's wearing her leather pants this morning? I've never thought of her as a-leather-and-chains person, but nothing would surprise me. Maybe we'll see a tattoo on her arm tomorrow to complete the look. Probably a butterfly. Yeah, I'm betting on a butterfly."

"Come on, Donna, leave the poor girl alone. If she gets a tattoo of any kind within the year, I'll take your Patrick to his hockey practices every Saturday morning for a month."

"Hey, you're on," said Donna delightedly. "I can talk her into getting one. I'll tell her it's the latest style—every female who's anybody in New York has a tattoo. That'll fetch her." I smiled to myself, remembering that Cyndi, who is really very conservative, had once confided her belief to me that people who tattooed themselves were basically insecure. I was confident that my Saturday mornings would remain free.

When Cyndi returned to the office struggling with a stepladder that she had found gawd-knows-where, we were both surprised when she brought it through to a spot on the floor beside my desk. We watched in silence as she went back to the front office, picked up the plant and chain, and came back in and mounted the ladder. Reaching the top and balancing herself and her burden carefully, she produced a curved hook from her pocket and reached up to put an end through one of the holes in the ceiling tile. She then fed the chain through the hook on the plant holder and the other end through the hook in the ceiling. She stepped down off the ladder and viewed her handiwork with satisfaction. "I'm so glad I had measured the length of chain I would need for hanging plants a while ago. I knew exactly how much to buy."

"Yes, it looks very nice," I said, stupefied.

"I thought you needed a plant in here," she said, smiling at me. "I'll water it for you and look after it." She folded up the ladder and departed once again.

Donna and I looked at the plant and at each other. "Okay, what's this all about?" she finally said. "I don't remember your mentioning that we wanted, liked, or could stand to have a plant hanging from our ceiling in here. What have you done to deserve this?"

"Beats me," I answered, "but you'll have to admit it looks quite attractive. And if she's going to look after it, why not?"

"No, the question is, why?"

I had nothing to say to that, and after a bit, Cyndi reappeared, having presumably returned the ladder, and shut the door between us in preparation for listening to the messages left on our voice mail, her first duty of the day. In time, she would come into our office with a number of them requiring a response from one of us, usually Donna.

About ten minutes later, all was revealed. Cyndi came to us with a handful of messages for Donna, and a package for me. "I really appreciate your offer of taking this blouse to Seatie," she said warmly. "Thank you so much."

"Oh, no problem," I said, glancing over at Donna who was pretending not to hear this exchange.

"Okay, talk to you later. Oh, by the way," turning at the door and motioning to the plant, "it's a spider plant."

"Ah. Thank you."

The door closed and Donna slumped over her desk, her shoulders shaking, and tears starting to stream down her face. I went back to my editing, knowing what she would likely say when she recovered, and she did.

"I can't think of a plant you would love more than that one. A spider plant," Donna hooted when she could finally talk. "So, will I have to listen to you scream when you walk in here every morning? That's what you get for doing Cyndi a favor."

I kept on working, not bothering to reply, but it didn't help. Over the next hour, Donna amused herself by calling out every few minutes, "Watch out for the spider (pause) plant!" No one would believe what I put up with when I'm trying to edit.

Later in the morning, Cyndi stuck her head in the office and announced, "Karl's here and wants to see you two."

"Call her back in and tell her we want him frisked for a knife before we'll listen to anything he has to say," Donna muttered. Too late. He was on Cyndi's heels, not waiting to see if we had time to talk to him or not.

"So, how are my favorite publishers who want to have 'MOR Dink'? Anything I can do to help?" he said, but without his usual enthusiasm. In fact, if I didn't know him better, I'd suspect our happy-go-lucky landlord was actually worried about something. Karl is in his mid-fifties but behaves like a young stud around women in spite of his sagging skin, a paunch, and serious hair loss.

"What we would really like is to have those steps fixed, Karl," Donna said, ignoring his stupid joke about the name of our company, which wasn't any funnier than the first hundred times he said it. "Every time someone comes up the stairs, it sounds like a banshee screeching. How much work is it to drive a couple of nails in them?"

"Yeah, yeah, I'll see to it," he responded as usual, approaching my desk, having chosen me as the lesser of the two evils in our office. "I wanted to make sure you got this notice about a visit from the Fire Department coming up next week. I take good care of my tenants, and I asked for an inspection to make sure the building was okay," he said, handing me a printed notice, which was a photocopy of the letter from the Fire Department announcing their annual inspection. He had no choice about agreeing to this, of course, and probably forgot that all his tenants would know that since all of us are able to read English and have at least a modicum of intelligence. He glanced suspiciously around the room, looking, no doubt, to see if we had built a bonfire on a slab of marble in the corner of the room to cook our lunch, or something. "This is the only notice you'll get. I don't know exactly which day the inspection will take place, but please cooperate." And he shot a meaningful glance at Donna, nodded to me, and departed.

"We took the portable fireplace out of here last month," Donna shouted after him. "Cyndi kept tripping over it."

"I wonder what's eating him," she remarked thoughtfully when he had banged the door behind him. "Only one snide comment about MORD Inc.? One lie? No personal insults? The man must be unwell."

"He's probably worried about the fire inspection. He's had two new tenants come into the building this year, and probably broke fifteen electrical wiring codes redesigning the offices and now needs to conceal the evidence," I said, tossing the notice aside.

"Either that or he's worried that his murder spree is about to come to an end. The cops are probably closing in on him," Donna said darkly. "He didn't even bring up the subject of the murder that took place in this very building, the building *he* owns? He's the perfect killer-type, you know. A big, blustery, con man. I don't know how his wife can stand him. He makes my flesh crawl."

"Actually, he's quite attractive in a big, blustery, con man sort of way," I said with a grin. "His poor wife was probably conned into believing he was a great catch and will come to her senses any day now. She's wife number three, and they haven't been married long. She could be busy right now trying to figure out what he's really worth.

"And speaking about 'worth,'" I continued, "as far as I'm concerned, we've got our money's worth out of that company sign and I'm going to make myself responsible for ripping it off the wall when I get a minute. I don't care what we paid for it; we really only need the name of the magazine on display. Enough is enough."

"As if Karl will ever forget the name," Donna said, "sign or no sign. We should sue that law student. The money we saved by going to him was eaten up by our having to get all our stationary reprinted, never mind what it will cost us to replace that sign."

"We can't sue him. He's probably a full-fledged lawyer by now and we wouldn't stand a chance," I said. "Anyway, it was just as much our fault that the name turned into a gross joke and you know it."

"I don't care. When I remember all the effort we put into making sure MORD Company and Mord Co. looked and sounded all right, I could strangle him," Donna said. "Maybe it was a good idea to become incorporated, but why didn't he realize how that would change the name? Lawyers are supposed to notice things like that. After we hung that expensive sign and said the name out loud, I almost puked."

"Except he wasn't a lawyer then," I reminded her. "And there was no danger of either of us puking; we were laughing too hard. It took us two days to recover. Forget about that and start worrying about what kind of firetrap we're working in. We have several days to go before the fire inspector makes Karl, the killer, rip out all the wiring downstairs and replace it with something approaching industry standards."

Donna made a face at me and we went back to work.

It was some time after lunch before I could break away from my office tasks and go over to The Manor to deliver the package for Cyndi. She told me Seatie's suite number and how to find her rooms on the first floor of the two-story building. One of the large double doors at the entrance of The Manor stood invitingly open and, once inside, I glanced to my right and saw into the office through large glass windows and the open door. A woman was inside with her back to me talking on the phone. In front of me was a large area with dining room tables and chairs, and a few comfortable-looking sofas under the stretch of windows that ran along the length of the room. A number of elderly people were seated in various parts of the room, and they looked at me with interest, but no one stopped me as I turned to my left and started down the long hall.

When I reached the number on the door that Cyndi had instructed me to find, I gave a little knock and wondered what I would do if Seatie didn't answer. She could be anywhere in the building, of course, or she might be napping. Didn't older people usually nap in the afternoon? I stopped quizzing myself when I heard someone inside fumbling with the doorknob, and finally the door opened wide to reveal a short, elderly woman, who was still pretty in spite of her advancing years. Her white, fluffy hair was thinning, but sparkling eyes in a round, attractive face peered at me expectantly. She was dressed nicely in a dark skirt and turquoise over-blouse, and small diamond earrings completed her outfit. This, of course, must be Seatie.

I introduced myself and told her my errand. She was very pleased and took the package happily. "Cyndi is such a sweet girl, and so are you for taking the time to deliver this for her," she said, beaming up at me. "I hope you have time to stop for a chat. Cyndi told me how wonderful it is to work at the magazine and how nice you people are. Such clever girls to publish a magazine all by yourselves!"

I suddenly felt like a teenager again and decided I needed to find some older friends who would continue to regard me as a youngster no matter how much I aged. I assured Seatie that I did have time for a chat and prepared to step into what appeared to be a combination kitchen-living room. Seatie quickly said, "No, no, not here, my dear. Let's go to the main room where we can have a cup of tea. Let me put this bag down somewhere, and then we can be off. I'm so glad to have my new blouse to wear for the special concert at dinner on Sunday." She peeked into the bag, smiling to herself, and then walked slowly over to the miniscule kitchen counter top and carefully placed the package down.

Her apartment was bright and cheerful, with an interesting mix of old and new furniture. There were cupboards above and below the kitchen counter and there was also a microwave oven, a two-burner hotplate, and a small refrigerator. Resting on the black-and-white floor tiles was a new, very small, round, wooden kitchen table with two matching chairs. Where the tiles ended, a gray, wall-to-wall carpet indicated the living room area. A bag of knitting rested against a recliner chair, which faced a contemporary wall unit complete with books, photographs, a television, and a radio and CD player. Under the window was a two-seater sofa for guests, and there were plants and flowers dotting the room. Everything was clean and neat and without the clutter that I usually associated with older people. Seatie must be ruthless about throwing out unnecessary items, but an old, small, glass-fronted china cabinet in the corner held some treasured dishes for which she likely had no use, but probably kept for sentimental reasons. There was a large bathroom opening off the kitchen area, and another open door to a bedroom disclosed a crazy quilt on a single bed and an old-fashioned dressing table covered with framed photographs.

"You must be comfortable here," I remarked, stepping out into the hall with Seatie and watched as she carefully locked the door behind her.

"Oh, yes, I am. I just love it here at The Manor." We made our way slowly up the hall to the dining-living room area that I passed on my way through the building and to which Seatie referred as the "main room." The sturdy little woman ignored the rails mounted waist-high along the walls that could be used to assist the frail and uncertain of step. "I'm eighty-eight," she announced, as though reading my thoughts, "but I can still get around without any difficulty."

"So, I see," I said, "and Cyndi tells me there are a lot of activities here to keep you active, busy, and entertained."

"My, yes, there are. I wish I could do more, in fact. I go to the exercise room to take part in armchair exercises three times a week, and I walk around outside the building every fine day. I also play bridge every other day. Yes, there are lots of fun things to do. This weekend, we have a choir from the high school coming to entertain us at dinner."

"How very nice," I said warmly, and meant it.

We reached the main room, and I noted that there were about twenty round dining room tables with six straight-backed armchairs at each; a high ceiling with a skylight; and the large windows stretching down the length of the room afforded a view of one of the gardens, a walkway, and a small pond. A few of the sofas placed under the windows were occupied and so were some of the chairs around the tables. Attractive, colorful paintings hung on the walls and the overall impression was of a bright, happy room, Seatie led the way to a large table at the end of the room which held coffee and hot water urns, milk, sugar, and tea bag containers, as well as cups and saucers, mugs, small plates, and a see-through covered bin holding an assortment of cookies, scones, and muffins. A large basket of fresh fruit served as the centerpiece.

Seatie paused at the snack table, and I poured myself a mug of coffee while she made herself a cup of tea. After she invited me to help myself to the available snacks, and I had politely refused, she chose a table close by and settled herself into one of the chairs. I selected another from which I could see the front door, which was now closed, the windowed office, two elevators near the office, and another stretch of hall leading to a second wing of the building.

While I was wondering how to tactfully introduce the topic of Jody or David or murder, a woman hesitantly approached our table.

"Here's Mrs. T," said Seatie happily. "Do join us, Dear. Mrs. T is my very good friend," she confided to me, "and her name is really Mrs. Theodore, but we all call her Mrs. T because it's so much more friendly-like."

Seatie made the formal introductions as Mrs. T seated herself in a chair beside her friend. Her acknowledgment of me included a faint smile. She looked younger than Seatie, probably in her late seventies, but was thin and pale. Perhaps her health wasn't good, and that is why she chose residence living. Her hair was a mixture of brown and white, and she wore pale pink lipstick. Like Seatie, she was nicely dressed and wore a few pieces of good jewelry, including a wedding ring. I wondered if there was a Mr. T.

"We've all been upset by what happened to Jody," Seatie said, turning to me. "How unfortunate that she was killed in your building—so disturbing for everyone who works there. And she was such a nice girl; we'll all miss her. I can't understand how a terrible thing like that can happen in our quiet neighborhood. All those thieves and killers let out on the street after serving so little time in prison—that must be the problem."

Mrs. T nodded her agreement to what must be the accepted theory among the residents to explain Jody's death.

"We were all shocked, too," I said, "and I guess Mrs. Parker and David were deeply affected by this dreadful tragedy, as well. Jody must have been a great help here."

"Oh, yes," said Seatie. "Jody arranged so many nice things for us and wonderful entertainment, and she worked so hard. We all loved her."

"Mrs. Parker didn't like her," Mrs. T said, looking off into the distance.

"Mrs. T!" Seatie exclaimed, looking slightly shocked.

"Well, she didn't," Mrs. T said with a shrug.

"We mustn't say such things," Seatie said primly. "It's not nice."

Mrs. T did not reply to this comment, but said, "There's David Parker now. His mother isn't here today."

Seatie and I looked to where she was gesturing and watched an undeniably handsome man emerge from the elevator and saunter over to the office where he stood in the doorway, leaning up against the frame and talking to someone inside. So, this was our David. He was tall and slim, around six foot, I estimated, and dressed appropriately in business casual, which, in this case, meant gray flannel, well-cut slacks, and an Italian knit sweater with a white collar showing above. With his rugged features and dark hair showing sprinkles of gray at the temples, he really was quite distractingly good-looking, and he was smiling as he moved away from the door and returned to the elevator. I couldn't suppress heaving a small sigh but at least I didn't disgrace myself by drooling.

"I guess Marianne must be on duty today, too, instead of Katherine. I saw Marianne in the office earlier," Mrs. T went on. "I'm sure David is relieved about that."

I assumed she meant that David would be pleased that his mother wasn't around and interfering, but I hesitated to ask for an explanation or to ask why Katherine didn't like Jody. Seatie so obviously disapproved of the subject, she might try to stop Mrs. T from answering. I decided to tackle the possible missing drug problem instead.

"The Manor seems to be so well run. I'm sure you all feel very secure here," I said. "Do you feel confident that your possessions are secure, too?"

Two surprised faces stared at me. "I mean," I said, fumbling for the right words, "do people here ever complain about losing articles from their apartments?"

"My Dear," Seatie said, "people complain about everything sooner or later and, yes, people complain about losing things all the time; however, it is usually their memories they are losing, not their possessions." Both women immediately broke into peals of laughter, and after a moment, I joined in.

"I can't find my memory anywhere," Mrs. T giggled, giving Seatie a poke in the ribs with her elbow, "have you seen it?" And Seatie pulled a dainty handkerchief from her pocket to dab at her eyes while she continued to laugh.

When the merriment died down, Seatie rose to her feet and announced that she was going to get herself a cookie. She was feeling a bit "peckish" she said. Both Mrs. T and I declined her offer to get something for us as well, and Seatie headed toward the snack table.

I decided to tackle Mrs. T head-on while I had the chance. "Why did Mrs. Parker not like Jody?"

Again, Mrs. T looked off into the distance. "Katherine thought David was sweet on Jody, and she was furious about it, as usual. She doesn't like anyone David is interested in and always tries to stop him from becoming involved. She's done it before. Oh, yes," and Mrs. T nodded to herself several times.

"Why is that?" I asked, but I had lost her.

"What is the name of that plant?" Mrs. T frowned at a large leafy plant in an attractive pot by the front entrance.

"I'm not sure. Did Mrs. Parker—Katherine—not want David to date an employee?"

"Oh, it wouldn't have mattered whether she was an employee or not. Any girl. She didn't want him to fall for any girl."

"Why not?"

"Are you sure you don't know what it's called? Someone told me the name once before but I can't remember it now," said Mrs. T, losing interest in my question once again.

"Perhaps she thought Jody wasn't good enough for her son," I said desperately trying to distract Mrs. T from her plant identification pursuit.

"No one would be good enough for her son," she replied dryly. "It might be a philodendron."

"Now, dear, I told you before, it's called a ficus," said Seatie, coming back to the table. Drat, the chance was gone.

"Oh, yes, that's right," said Mrs. T absently.

I decided to mention the courier. "I guess the police were here to see if anyone knew the courier who was killed around the same time as Jody."

"Jody wouldn't waste her time on a courier," announced Mrs. T still staring intently at the ficus plant as though she thought it might suddenly climb out of the planter and slink off down the hall.

I had nothing to say to that, but Seatie promptly replied, "Oh, I am sure the poor man's murder had nothing to do with Jody. The Manor always uses UPS couriers. I see the truck here every day, and so Jody wouldn't have met a Hasty Xpress courier. That is, she wouldn't have met him working here," she corrected herself, "although she could have become acquainted with him somewhere else, of course. It's a great pity this isn't a murder mystery, or we would know who all the suspects are."

"Oh, do you read murder mysteries, too? I really love them," I smiled at her.

"I do, I do," Seatie responded enthusiastically. "I have a great collection of murder mysteries—all the Agatha Christie books and all those written by Dick Francis, and lots of others."

"I like both of those writers, as well. Another favorite mystery author of mine is Mary Roberts Rinehart. Do you like her writing?"

"I don't believe I've read her. Are her books good?"

"Yes, if you like Agatha Christie, you'd like Rinehart. I'll lend you one of mine," I offered, thinking I could use another excuse to come over to The Manor, and that would be as good as any.

"How sweet of you. Thank you so much. Isn't she sweet?" Seatie said, turning to Mrs. T.

Mrs. T turned a slightly vacant look towards her and smiled. "I've always liked *I Love Lucy*," she said.

"That's a TV show, not a book," Seatie reproved her gently.

"Yes, but I like it anyway," was the answer.

"I wonder if Jody has any family in town," I said.

"Her mother lives in Vancouver and that's where the funeral will be held this Saturday. Katherine and Marianne are going to attend, and so are a few other people from The Manor. There will be good representation from here and I am sure her mother will be pleased. We've all contributed to buy some beautiful flowers for the poor child," Seatie said comfortably.

I greeted this news with respectful silence and digested the fact that I wasn't going to find out anything about David, missing drugs, or Jody's personal life on this visit.

"Our magazine is going run an article about your beautiful residence in one of our upcoming issues," I said, deciding to change the topic.

"How lovely," exclaimed Seatie at the same time that Mrs. T said, "What a nice idea," and they both smiled delightedly at me.

Since this announcement had captured their interest, I made a decision on the spot. "We'll have someone take a couple of pictures to illustrate the story and perhaps you two would like to be in one of them."

They were both pleased with that idea and I knew I had paved the way for any subsequent visits I might want to make. Besides, we really would want some residents in one of the pictures, at least, and these were two nice-looking women who would photograph well.

There were smiles and thank you's all around when I finally finished my coffee and excused myself to go back to work. I hadn't learned much this time, but perhaps another visit to The Manor would prove to be more fruitful. At least I had laid the groundwork.

The rest of the day passed fairly quietly, except for the arrival of an article about the new slate of officers elected to the Chamber of Commerce. It was such a badly written piece of junk, its arrival deserves mention as one of the memorable events of the day. I was going to have to completely rewrite the thing, as if I didn't have enough to do.

I was less than happy to leave work at five o'clock as I was falling too far behind with my ads and editing even though it meant that I now arrived home at a decent hour for dinner. Could enjoying an early dinner be the reason most people tended to show up for work at eight or nine in the morning and leave work at five or six? I considered the theory as I began pulling dinner possibilities out of the fridge, and decided that nothing was really worth giving up that extra half-hour in bed in the morning, not even an early dinner. Come to think of it, I wasn't even particularly hungry. I settled on a ham-stuffed pepper, added a side salad and a glass of Chianti to the meal—not so unusual for me—and dessert, which *was* unusual for me. I cast a loving eye on the glorious chunk of chocolate cake that I'd had the presence of mind to pick up from the bakery on my way home.

After dinner was over and I had eaten the last crumb of cake, I knew I couldn't put off my evening task any longer. I flipped through my notebook and glanced at the questions I had prepared for the actuarial/accountant article that Donna had coerced me into writing. The next step was to go over and knock on Stuart's door and ask him if I could interview him for an article about his company—as soon as I cleared up the dishes, of course. I dilly-dallied over this small domestic chore as I mentally squirmed over the ifs and buts I would have to include in my approach to him. We would use the article in December if The Manor article doesn't run ... if Stuart wouldn't mind explaining the way in which actuaries and accountants work together so that we could use the article to sell ads to accounting companies ... but if the article didn't run in the December issue, we would use it in another issue... but we need to prepare it right away, just in case ... blah, blah, blah. I wasn't good at this stuff and I knew it.

When I couldn't think of any more excuses to delay, I tidied myself up and walked across the hall to Stuart's apartment. Maybe he wouldn't be home tonight, I thought hopefully, as I tapped on the door. Maybe I was in the wrong line of work. I suspect that a good editor would be happy to arrange interviews, and I found myself wishing that Donna could have orchestrated this one. She loved talking to people and would have had Stuart eating out of her hand in no time. Donna often made the arrangements for my interviews, leaving me only the job of fixing a date and time.

I had already started to back away from the door when it suddenly opened and Stuart was there in front of me. Of medium height and weight, Stuart had gray hair, slightly receding from his forehead, dark brown eyes, and a pleasant face. He was wearing a sweatshirt, blue jeans, and bedroom slippers, and gave me a welcoming, if surprised, smile. I stumbled through my explanation of the article I wanted to write, apologizing with every second sentence. Stuart's smile widened when he finally figured out what I was proposing and said, "I'd love to do it. Do you want to interview me tonight?"

A great wave of relief washed over me, and I said, "Sure, whenever you are ready. Why don't you come over to my apartment? I have some questions prepared."

"All right, I'll be over in about ten minutes." We smiled at each other and I scurried back to my place and put my notebook and pens on the table. I prepared a pot of coffee, and after a minute of thought, put two wine glasses as well as two coffee mugs on the kitchen counter, and the bottle of Chianti I had opened at dinner.

Stuart made his appearance, his slippers replaced with casual shoes, in less than ten minutes, and I was all ready for him. I offered him the choice of coffee or a glass of wine, and he chose the wine. I poured us each a glass, and we settled ourselves at the table. Stuart answered my questions easily without any sign of self-consciousness. He was articulate and funny, and I was impressed.

"So, an actuary's work is really all about future risk assessment? Is that the best way to describe it?" I asked as we were winding down.

"Yes, but be sure and include the fact that mathematics is the tool we use. We don't want anyone confusing us with soothsayers and fortune tellers," he smiled.

I assured him that I would do my best not to mislead our readers on that point and promised that I would give him the article to read before publication. "How helpful is this skill to you personally?" I asked, closing my notebook. "Can you calculate the odds on being successful at something you do, or the likelihood of your dying in the next year?"

Stuart shook his head. "Mortality charts are available for anyone to look at, and like everyone else, I can look up the age at which most men die who were born the same year I was, but actuarial science is designed to deal with large groups of people, not individuals. I could live for many years past the time that most males in my cohort die, or I could have died in my first year of life. As well, the likelihood of winning a lottery ticket is remote, but, of course, someone does win, and how predictable was that for the individual who won? The winner beat the odds."

"It's a pretty fascinating subject," I said, getting up to bring the bottle of Chianti to the table. "I wish you could use it to tell me what the odds are of the police solving the murder of the woman who was killed in our building, and the death of the courier murdered within hours that same day."

"I wish I could, too," Stuart replied seriously. "Do the police think the two murders are related? The newspapers hinted that they might be."

"I haven't heard anything about it, but I am sure the police are investigating the possibility and one link is that both victims were killed in the same manner."

"It must be making everyone in your building quite anxious. I understand that you and your business partner actually found the body of the woman. That must have been exceedingly unpleasant. Did you know her?"

"Only by sight, and yes, it was unpleasant," I said, topping up our wine glasses, "and the police demanded alibis although neither of us had formally met Jody, who was the manager of the seniors' residence next door to our office building."

"I hope you had a good one."

"The best. I was busy disgracing myself in a restaurant full of people at the time she must have been killed." And I told him about my encounter with the spider.

Stuart laughed and then looked serious. "Has this sort of thing happened to you many times in public? There are an awful lot of spiders around."

"It's happened a few times. I was embarrassed the first time, but I was only ten years old. The next time, I was eighteen, and at a picnic with a group of university students. Everyone was sympathetic. They were all aware that they were seeing a full-blown phobia, no matter what they thought of my particular fear. All the psych students probably ran off as soon as they could to make notes on the whole thing. My date killed the spider and felt very proud of himself, doing the macho thing and rescuing the maiden in distress. Everyone was so kind and so interested in my fear, I stopped feeling embarrassed. Finally, I did a little basic research and found that fear of spiders—arachnophobia—is listed right after fear of snakes as one of the top ten phobias."

"But fear of snakes is more understandable. A lot of snakes can kill people. How many spiders can do that?"

"Not many, but what harm can a garter snake do? People afraid of snakes are just as afraid of a little garter snake as they are of boa constrictors or rattlesnakes. Everyone is afraid of a poisonous snake or a poisonous spider. That is perfectly normal and makes sense. What isn't normal and doesn't make sense is to be afraid of all snakes or all spiders, dangerous or not. That's called a phobia."

"Have you ever tried to do anything about it?"

"You mean take therapy?" I asked.

"Yes."

"I did try something on my own once," I said, sipping my wine. "I decided to deal with it when I was about twelve or thirteen by educating myself about spiders. I thought that might do it. I armed myself with the appropriate volume of our encyclopedia, and a couple of *National Geographic* magazines with articles and pictures about spiders and their habitats. I had noticed a big, red spider ensconced on a web, safely outside the window just above the sofa and it triggered off my plan. I decided to read all about spiders, study the pictures, and then sit and stare at the spider outside and try to appreciate its beauty," I said, warming to the topic. "Of course, I didn't know about phobias at the time, and didn't understand why I was so afraid. It was a real problem for me when I worked in the garden, which was one of my chores, and I was ashamed of my fear and wanted to do something about it."

"So, what happened?" asked Stuart, looking genuinely interested—and I hoped he really was and that I wasn't boring him to death.

"It all went beautifully at first," I said. "Then came the part where I was kneeling on the sofa, staring at the spider outside, and saying something to myself in the nature of, 'It's so beautiful. It's a beautiful color, and it has spun a beautiful web. Look at its dainty legs. This is a beautiful insect.' I kept repeating whatever it was to myself like a litany; and then, without warning, the spider suddenly darted up its web. I screamed and threw myself backward off the sofa and landed on the floor. My Dad, who worked at a tire plant, was on night shift that week and had been asleep for about three hours. He came tearing out of the bedroom in his pajamas, yelling, 'What happened? What happened?' I told him I had been frightened by a big spider. He knew all about my fear, and asked, 'Where is it?' I pointed to the window where he could see the spider outside. 'Jeeze,' he said in disgust, and stomped back into the bedroom, slamming the door behind him. I was relieved he never told my mother, who was out at the time. She would have been annoyed with me if she knew I had woken him up and why. I decided not to try anything like that again."

Stuart smiled and shook his head. "You once mentioned having a younger sister that you raised like a daughter. Was she with you when she was small? Did she ever see you react like that?"

"She was ten when she came to live with us and, no, I always managed to stay calm whenever Mandy was around and I had to dispose of a spider. I really didn't want to make her afraid of them and she never saw me jump and scream when one of them got too close, and I was lucky about that, I guess. What happened in the restaurant the other day was pretty unusual. However, my masterful self-control didn't help at all and Mandy's afraid of spiders, too. It's a common fear, and I swear I didn't impose that on her. I understand a recent theory is that such fears are carried in our DNA. I put the blame on one of my ancestors who was probably bitten by a poisonous spider and became horribly ill. Mandy never saw me overreact; I know she didn't."

Stuart nodded. "Whatever the cause of your fear, the only other thing you could do is take some genuine therapy. Self-help techniques can only get you so far and, in your case, haven't seemed to have gotten you anywhere at all. However, there are worse phobias to have."

"Right. At the moment, I think I'm developing a phobia about murder, which I also don't expect to encounter very often. I wish I knew what was going on and who the suspects are, and whether the murder of the courier was connected to Jody's murder or not."

"Yes, I'm sure you are concerned about that. Are you likely to know some of the suspects personally? Are the police looking closely at the people in your building because one of the murders took place there?"

"I'm not sure who the police are considering, and I guess I am mostly concerned about one man who seems to have come to the attention of the police. He's a friend of a friend," I added hastily, suddenly remembering that I was hoping to cultivate a romance between Donna my very nice neighbor. It would hardly do to describe Donna as having a schoolgirl crush on one of the murder suspects.

Stuart nodded again. "I think the only thing anyone besides the police can do at this point is keep an eye out for the common denominator. That's usually an indication."

Maybe it was the wine, but I wasn't sure what he meant, and I decided it was probably time to lighten up the conversation: "I've remembered that I need something else from you for the article."

"What's that?"

"A suitable joke. Give me an actuarial joke that I can use."

He thought a moment. "Okay, this one is pretty good: Actuaries can tell you how many people are going to die each year; Sicilian actuaries can give you their names and addresses."

"I love it," I laughed.

"On the other hand, you may upset the sensibilities of your Sicilian readers. I'd better try to dig up another one for you."

"That's probably a good idea, but I'd love to print that one."

"I'd better be running along now," Stuart said, glancing at his watch, and standing up. "Thank you for the wine and the interview. I'll look forward to reading your article, and I hope I talked enough about accountants that you will be able to sell lots of ads around it."

"You are very welcome, and thank you so much for rescuing us," I said, giving him my best smile.

We said our goodnights, and he left, and it wasn't until I was clearing the wineglasses from the table that it occurred to me I should have offered him either red or white wine. I did have a Chardonnay in the refrigerator. Oh, well, he drank a second glass of the red Chianti—he couldn't have minded it too much even if it wasn't his favorite. In any case, I had the information for my article. All in all, it was a good evening. Stuart was such a thoroughly nice man. Perfect for Donna.

-8-

Friday unfolded as Fridays always do with everyone at the office upbeat and looking forward to the weekend, now within reach. Even a couple of murders hanging over our heads didn't dampen the mood.

Donna bounced into the office after her meeting at The Manor with David and handed me his ad with a flourish. "Here's the full-page ad, and he'll run it again with the article whenever we publish it! What do you say about that? And Katherine has agreed to the interview. So, we may still have the article for the December issue. Katherine is at the office now, and you are supposed to call her and schedule a time. David was on his way out after our meeting, but I guess Katherine will know when they are both available."

"Congratulations. A whole-page ad is great, and if David is prepared to run it again, all the better. Good for you!"

"It wasn't my amazing powers of persuasion. David had already decided that he wanted a big ad in the next two issues. He told me they have a few vacancies at the moment, and considering the publicity they have had over the murder of one of their managers, he wants to do a little damage control. He also took the time to show me around the residence. It's really very nice."

I refused to ask any questions about David. "I know. I saw it yesterday, remember? It's a great place. Imagine never have to cook and clean again. I've already reserved a room. I'm considering moving in next week."

"Forget it. You'd never make it to breakfast in time and all that money would be wasted," said Donna. "By the way, I have to go out again and have our customers sign off on the ads you finished, which I assume they have already approved. I won't be back until after lunch; I'm meeting my friend, Sharon, at the Steak House. It's pizza night for our family and so I'm fueling up."

"Yes, I heard back from everyone and all the ads are approved. I'm working through my lunch hour today, but I'm leaving early. I plan to be out of here by two-thirty at the latest."

"That's right, you're driving to Nanaimo for the weekend, aren't you? Well, if you're gone before I get back, have a good time. I'll see you bright and early Monday morning," Donna said with a grin, "whether you like it or not."

"I don't like it, but I'll be here. Enjoy yourself at Patrick's bright-and-early Saturday hockey practice at—what is it?—seven in the morning, did you say?"

"Hah! I can't wait for Cyndi to get her tattoo and don't forget to call Katherine." And she was gone.

I reached for the phone after checking The Manor number on the ad, and Katherine answered on the first ring. She was brisk and pleasant. We made arrangements to meet Monday afternoon, and Katherine told me that David would see me early Wednesday morning. How early? "About eight-thirty or nine o'clock," Katherine suggested. I opted for the nine o'clock appointment and hung up feeling that I was gradually losing control of my life. Is the whole world full of mad people who leap happily out of bed at the break of dawn?

When the hour to leave the office finally arrived, it felt good to close down my computer for the weekend. I had finished the first draft of my possible lead article for December with the information Stuart had given me; Cyndi was hard at work; Donna was due to come back and finish off the day; and the parking lot was still full of cars awaiting the drones in the Ullman Building to come and retrieve them. My extended weekend was all the sweeter knowing that the time was stolen from the regular workday. I firmly pushed the worry about my workload right out of my mind.

As I drove up to my apartment building, Ryan and Hogg were in the parking lot, and I gave them a wave. Ryan was still some distance away, but he paused, leaning up against a car, and waited for me as I climbed out and locked my car door. As I drew near, he called out:

"He dropped his joint in a coffee cup.

The coffee cup was filled to brim;

'God' Ned thought, 'My life is grim,'

His mouth dissolving in a pout,

He shuddered as he fished it out."

I laughed and gave him a thumbs-up. He turned away with a smile and ambled off in the direction Hogg had taken. Ryan's beautiful golden hair was trimmed, but still long, and he had a new backpack slung over his shoulder. I wondered if he and Hogg were now living in the apartment in our building that had been vacated recently. I guessed I'd soon find out.

I hurried into the building and to my apartment where I threw things into an overnight bag. I packed a book on animals that I had picked up for Josh, along with two little toy dinosaurs. I didn't know what kind they were, but Josh would. I also found room for some recent photos, and a new magazine that I thought would interest Mandy. Quickly changing into comfortable jeans and a dark green turtleneck, I grabbed my tweed jacket and the overnight bag, and headed out.

I wove my way through Victoria's traffic until I reached the Island highway and was on my way with a relatively clear road ahead of me. I had gassed up the car last night after work; I had Nick Cave on CD to entertain me on the trip, and if I wanted to change from rock to folk, Gordon Lightfoot was waiting in the wings.

The sun was shining, but not too brightly, and the traffic wasn't bad yet, but I knew there would be many more cars on the road in another couple of hours. I tried to relax and enjoy the weather, the scenery, and the music, but this was always a difficult trip for me to make—it was on this highway that we had the accident and Don had lost his life when he was much too young. In the nine years since then, a lot of changes had been made to the road. Stretches of the highway were now wider and straighter, and there were new lanes added in many sections of it as well, and it was now called "the new highway." Not only were there man-made changes to the road, nature had also altered the look of the route. Small trees had grown large; bushes had expanded. I was no longer able to identify exactly where our car had gone off the road, and for that I was grateful. I knew that the section might now be part of "the old highway" and I wasn't even traveling on it anymore. Nevertheless, ever since that night, the horror and shock of the accident hung there in the back of my mind every time I climbed into a car as either a driver or a passenger. How I had escaped with only minor injuries after being thrown from the car is still a mystery to me, but here I am, many years later, with only a few faint scars on my body but sufficient scars in my mind that kept me wishing I didn't have to travel anywhere by car. I knew this drive offered spectacular Island scenery, but, for the most part, I kept my eyes firmly fixed on the road.

I suppose if I ever wanted to feel comfortable traveling by car, I should go into therapy—therapy for my spider fear, as Stuart had suggested, and my car-travel fear. Was there anything else? Maybe I could come up with a few more problems and take care of everything at once. How about my hatred of getting up early in the morning? My difficulty falling asleep before midnight? My dislike of setting up interview appointments? My aversion to sauerkraut? My inability to take that final step in my stop-smoking plan? I could keep a whole team of therapists busy for years.

I entertained myself for a while by mentally naming everything I feared and disliked and managed to do it all to the beat of Nick's music. Occasionally, my eyes flicked to my rear view mirror and, in time, I became aware of a dark van following one or two cars behind. I assumed there were a few vehicles traveling at the same speed as I was, and I had good reason to follow the rules of the road.

I pushed the thoughts of car accidents out of my mind, and turned my attention to speculation about our busy little killer. After a few moments of this unpleasant and unproductive activity, I turned the CD player off and the radio on. The harmless banter of two disk jockeys coupled with music from the sixties worked its magic, until I looked back and saw the same dark van—black, I noted—still on my heels, never getting closer than one or two cars.

I decided to nip this fear in the bud and took the first exit that appeared after rounding a curve. I watched my rear view window and was relieved that the only vehicle taking the same exit was a delivery truck, white, with painted illustrations of bakery products. Unfortunately, with trees blocking most of the highway, I missed seeing the black van at all. I pulled over, got out of the car and, leaning up against it, smoked a cigarette and watched the highway through a small gap in the trees. There was nothing of interest to be seen. I turned my attention to the dazzling fall colors all around me that I missed on the drive, unable to take my eyes off the road. When I stubbed out the remains of my cigarette, I got into the car and back on the highway, and continued my journey, safe from whatever murderous thugs may have been driving the black van, which I never saw again.

I arrived in Nanaimo in a contented frame of mind. Mandy and Josh were my two favorite people in the world, and I would have no responsibilities for the next couple of days other than entertaining Josh, which was an easy job.

Mandy and Josh were waiting at the door of their townhouse when I finally pulled into the driveway, and Josh flew into my arms.

"We're going to eat at a restaurant, Aunt Rachel," he announced joyfully as I hugged him and then Mandy.

"I know, I know," I said to my happy little nephew, "and I brought something for you to enjoy while we are waiting for our food to be served." I produced the book and the dinosaurs for Josh, and the photos and magazine for Mandy, and then walked into the tiny guestroom and dropped my overnight bag with a blissful sigh. It was going to be a good weekend.

We were at the restaurant waiting for our food and Josh was engaged with his new book when Mandy dropped her bombshell. "You know the incident that occurred at your building," she began, with a nod towards Josh, reminding me that the subject in question was not to be named, "there have been articles in our newspaper about it, and in the Victoria *Times-Colonist* as well. There were quite a few photos in the papers, and I recognized the woman—Jody. Later, I recognized someone associated with the event when I saw him interviewed on television. I saw the two of them together not long ago."

"Really?" I said. "Who was it?"

"The owner of your building. The reporters were asking him questions about the incident in his building to which his only reply was, 'No comment,' but the camera was on him long enough for me to recognize him."

"You saw Karl Ullman with Jody? Recently? Where? Here?" The questions tumbled out in my astonishment.

"No, they were at a cozy little restaurant in an Inn near Parksville a couple of weeks ago, and behaving in a very cozy little manner. My guess is that they are more than good friends."

"That is extremely interesting news. I haven't heard anything about that—not even a hint from anyone. I wonder if the pol ... our friends in blue know that tidbit. Do you remember the name of the Inn? Oh, and, not that it's important, but who were you with at this cozy little Inn?"

Mandy grimaced. "Dream on. I was with my friend Heather and we were pricing a job in Parksville. I took her with me because the clients needed an architect to draw up some changes they wanted made to the house and, afterwards, Heather and I went to this neat place for a late dinner. She had been there before and it's a bit off the beaten path. I can't remember the name at the moment, but I have the business card at home."

"Good. I can think of some people who would be interested," I said. At that point, our meal arrived, and we turned to subjects of interest to Josh, who was happy to see the food and to join the conversation. The time passed pleasantly, and I was quizzing Josh on what he had learned in kindergarten about animals—an amazing amount, I realized, which left me resolving to expand my own animal knowledge-base before he discovered my ignorance—when Mandy interrupted.

"Here comes a friend of ours, Dodie Boucher," and then added in an undertone to me, "She's a psychic, and really fun and nice. You'll like her."

I looked with interest at the woman who had smilingly abandoned her companions and the waiter leading them towards the staircase and was making her way through the tables towards us. She was about my age, very tall, with long, dark brown hair turning gray and pulled back into a braid. She wore no makeup and was dressed attractively in an embroidered skirt, white blouse and a colorful patchwork jacket. It was exactly the kind of outfit I liked and would have loved to wear if I hadn't already tried something similar and discovered that it made me look like a bag lady. She, however, looked like an artist, or someone interesting, at least. I wondered if the "psychic" would ask me my astrological sign, and I tried frantically to remember it.

"Well, it's the Campbells out for a night on the town," she said. "Hi, Mandy; hello, Josh." Dodie smiled at me and waited for Mandy to introduce us, which she did. I learned that her name was Dorothy, but everyone called her Dodie.

"I'm so glad to meet you, at last," she said to me. "Mandy talks about you all the time. You have such an interesting job; I envy you."

I made the usual sort of response and wondered if I should ask what work she did. Mandy saved me from having to decide by asking Dodie how her shop was doing.

"Very well, thank you. People are buying a lot of potted herbs now that most gardens have been harvested and put to bed for the winter, and I have a big market for my dried herbs as well."

Interesting. Maybe "psychic" was the politically correct term for "witch."

"So you have an herb shop?" I asked.

"Herbs and flowers, and seedlings, too, in the spring—plus other odds and ends. I have a great time with my shop. Something interesting is always happening, and the customers are such fun."

She gave me a piercing look. "You've been having some trouble lately, haven't you?"

"Yes, that's true. There have been some disturbing things happening in my life," I said, feeling a bit uncomfortable, and then suddenly remembering with relief that my astrological sign was Pisces in case the subject came up. I added firmly, "However, I'm going to forget all about it for the weekend. I'm here to have some fun, and Josh and I have a lot of plans."

"That's wonderful. Lucky Josh." She turned and smiled at him. "I can't believe how you've grown, Josh. You look so much taller than you did early in the summer."

Josh, of course, was very pleased to hear that, and told her exactly how tall he was, and added his weight, too, in case that was cause for more congratulations, which it was.

And then, "Don't worry," she said, nodding to me, "everything will become clear very soon. You and your friend are quite safe."

I was struck dumb, of course, but she had looked away and announced that she must join her friends. Mandy, Josh and I gave her a chorus of goodbyes, and I added that it was nice to have met her and she left us. I wouldn't have liked to go searching for anyone in this restaurant—a converted old house with rooms rambling all over the place—but perhaps her psychic powers told her exactly where she would find her friends. I looked questioningly at Mandy, but she shook her head and said, "More later."

That night, after we tucked Josh into bed and I had read him a story, we took a tour through the house and I admired all the latest decorative touches Mandy had added since my last visit. She really was gifted in this field, I thought with pleasure, as I stood looking down at one of her simple arrangements with pinecones and twigs in a glass bowl on an ochre-painted sideboard. New throw cushions in cheerful fabric had been added to her remarkably comfortable sofa. I was happy that she had returned to work in an area in which she was so obviously talented.

We finally donned jackets and retired to the back patio to enjoy the starlit night and crisp fall air. Mandy had made a good choice in selecting this townhouse for their new home. The units were well designed with no noise able to penetrate the walls and, as they were two-story units in a two-story building, it was quiet overhead as well. The patio fencing, covered in ivy, separated them from neighbors on both sides, and a thick hedge along the back gave them privacy as well as safety. There was a small round table and chairs for eating outside, a barbeque, and fragrant herbs, vines, and flowers spilling out of attractive pots at various heights.

I glanced over at Mandy, visible from the light filtering through the curtains of the house. She looked a bit weary, but as pretty as ever. She had our mother's blonde hair, our father's gray eyes, and a flawless complexion. At twenty-eight, she also had a lovely figure, which, as far as I knew, she maintained without any effort at all.

"So, how are things going?" I asked, meaning with Elliot, which she understood immediately. They had been separated for about a year now, and she didn't talk much about what had happened, falling back on that useful phrase "irreconcilable differences." Actually, that phrase gave me quite a bit of hope that the differences were not irreconcilable, and that the two of them would eventually be able to work things out. If the relationship really were hopeless, she would have spilled all. The fact that she didn't complain about how impossible he was to live with and name specific flaws made me believe that she didn't want to give me any ammunition to dislike him if and when they patched things up. In any case, I was already aware of a number of his flaws and would have found him impossible to live with myself, but, then, I wasn't Mandy. As far as I knew, the big trigger for the split was Mandy's insistence that she was going back to work full time. Elliot couldn't seem to adjust to that idea and clung to the notion that he deserved a wife who cooked, cleaned, and provided him with valet services. Hard to understand how any man under the age of ninety could believe such miracles existed in this day and age.

She shrugged. "We're in touch," she said. "He's very good about calling Josh almost every other day and takes him for weekends twice a month. He would like to have him more frequently but, with traveling so much, he really can't manage it. His recent promotion to pharmaceutical sales manager for the province means that he travels more than ever. Our arrangement is probably better for Josh right now, anyway. He loves his dad but, at five years old, he's much closer to me, of course. Maybe we can manage something different when he's older and it will be important for him to spend more time with his dad."

I agreed and changed the subject. "So, tell me about your friend Dodie. I would have been more impressed with what she said to me—obviously referring to the murders in Victoria—if I wasn't aware that she probably saw the name of the magazine or my name in a newspaper article, or remembered where your sister worked. I was a bit shocked that she mentioned it in the way that she did."

"Oh, don't misunderstand. She probably didn't realize the significance of what she said herself. Normally, she reads palms—the lines on the hand, you know? But in addition, she does other psychic stuff. I don't really understand it, and she doesn't talk much about it. Once, when she said something odd to me, I asked her what made her say that—it was right out of the blue. She said the thought came into her mind, and there was some urgency attached to it. She knew that she should tell me. She says that she has learned to go ahead and say whatever she thinks when that happens. Quite often, the person to whom she is speaking realizes exactly what she means even though it may not make sense to her."

"And did you understand what she meant at the time? And how can she take such a chance if she doesn't know what she's talking about?"

"I understood what she said, although I am not sure if what she said is true. And I think she understands what she is talking about all right, but she doesn't necessarily understand its significance. She told me that when she was younger, she often didn't speak those thoughts aloud, and would later learn what something meant and, in every instance, she was sorry that she hadn't spoken. So now, she always does—in case it matters; in case it's important. And, hey, what she said to you was important to me. I'm glad to hear that you and Donna are safe."

"Well, of course we're safe. I've never worried about that," I said, crossing my fingers, knowing that she couldn't see them in the dark. "I was more interested in hearing that 'all would be clear soon.' I guess that means the police are about to arrest the culprit. Maybe she's picking up the thoughts of one of the cops in Victoria."

"I have no idea how she does whatever she does. Anyway, I haven't got around to it yet, but I've been considering asking her to read my palm sometime."

"You really do believe she can read the future?" I said, surprised.

"I don't believe it or disbelieve it; I don't know. Have you absolutely ruled out the possibility of someone being able to tell you about yourself and the possibilities in your future by reading your palm?"

"I haven't ruled it out; I really haven't thought much about it," I admitted. "The idea that someone could actually do that disturbs me a bit because I don't like the idea that someone who doesn't know me could predict what I am likely to do and what is likely to happen to me."

"I don't believe that's quite it. It seems to me that it's more along the lines of her telling you what choices you have in your future. You still have to make them. Anyway, I am going to have her do a reading for me when I can find the time. I'll let you know what I think after I have it done."

"You do that," I said, hiding my smile.

"By the way, I bought a book for you to read while you're here. I was at a book fair last weekend and I found one that will be perfect for you."

"A murder mystery?"

"No, it's all about how to keep yourself safe. Not only in your apartment, but on the street."

"Oh, right, I'm in a lot of danger on the street. Last week, I saw a strange-looking man on the street but, luckily, I managed to get away."

"You can go ahead and joke, but wait until you've read what this writer has to say. The author is a psychologist who has treated many victims of violent attacks. After what happened this past week, you ought to be interested. I read a bit of it and looked at the chapter titles, and it looks to me that it might be worth reading. Did you bring anything to read this weekend?"

"No, I knew I would have access to all your books."

"Well, they are off limits until you read at least the first couple of chapters of this one. I bought it especially for you."

Her voice was even, but I caught an undertone. It suddenly occurred to me that she was a woman living alone, too, and responsible for the care of a young child. Perhaps it was her safety or Josh's safety she was worried about. Or maybe she really was worried about me. She had neighbors close by and good friends but, aside from little Josh, I was her only family— unless Elliot came back into the picture. When she came to live with me after our mother died, I was married and so she acquired Don as a father or big brother, and then we both lost him. It was a lot for her to carry, and for me as well.

I reached out and touched her hand. "Thank you. I'll be glad to read it; I'll start it tonight."

Her relief was unmistakable. "Good. I've left the book on your bedside table. I'm going to take myself to bed really early tonight and I know how late you are likely to stay awake. Read in the living room if you would be more comfortable, and I've set out some wine if you want a nightcap. It's on the kitchen counter."

"I spotted it, thanks. What time do you have to get up?"

"I have to catch the early ferry and so I'll probably be up by five o'clock. I'll try not to wake you. Josh will probably sleep until seven-thirty or maybe even eight. You know where everything is, right?"

"Of course. Don't worry about a thing. I'm going to take Josh to the Nanaimo District Museum and then to the park. You haven't been to the museum with him recently, have you?"

"The last time we went was when you took us," Mandy said, "and I recall that he loved it. He'll be thrilled."

The conversation drifted on to such details as meal options and where I could find Josh's boots and rain gear in case we needed it. We established the fact that Mandy would be coming back on the last ferry which meant Josh wouldn't see her at all as she would arrive home after ten o'clock tomorrow night. I would probably have time to finish reading the book if I started it tonight, and could take it home with me if I didn't.

After we had exhausted these mundane topics, Mandy asked me for a recap of what I knew about the murders, what I believed, what Donna guessed, and whom Donna and I suspected, if anyone. She was amused when I told her that we had arbitrarily decided to suspect Karl simply because we didn't like him. Mandy's news that Jody and Karl appeared to be friends, never mind "more than good friends," may or may not be known by the police yet, and I made it clear that I planned to tell them. His involvement might not be the joke Donna and I thought it was.

"I hope that doesn't mean I will be called as a witness or anything," she said.

"No, it means the police will go to the Inn at which you and Heather spotted them, armed with names and pictures, and start working on finding out more about their relationship. That is assuming they don't know about it already. Karl will have a bit of explaining to do if he hasn't told them, but that doesn't make him guilty of anything but adultery—if you read the situation right—and it certainly doesn't mean that he killed anyone. The police are used to having people withhold information even when they aren't guilty of a serious offence. However, it establishes a motive for Jody being in the building and, if Karl happened to be there at the same time—and I don't know about that—the police will certainly want to take a good look at him."

Mandy shuddered. "Can you imagine not only knowing two people who were murdered, but also knowing the murderer personally? That's too dreadful for words."

"Since people are usually murdered by someone who knows them, it stands to reason that other acquaintances will know everyone involved," I answered dryly. "In fact, statistically speaking, you are most likely to be murdered by a family member. Think about that the next time you invite me for a visit."

"Rachel! That's horrible!"

"I know. Why don't we talk about something else? Let me tell you about Donna's new love interest instead," I said, and launched into a colorful description of David, and Donna's schoolgirl crush. I told her that David was an accountant and carefully eliminated the name of the place where David worked and the fact that he had become an object of interest to the police after Jody's murder. Mandy knew Donna almost as well as I did, liked her as much, and giggled in all the right places. When she stood up and announced that she had to get some sleep, I was pleased to note that she was in a much happier frame of mind. We gave each other a goodnight hug, and Mandy went off to bed and I went off to do my assigned reading.

The book wasn't as disturbing as I feared, although some of the descriptions of how people, especially women, had been selected for attack were certainly alarming. The point the author was making was that people are usually oblivious to danger and become targets for violent crime as a result. I thought about what I did when I saw a van parked by a sidewalk when I was walking towards it, which was basically nothing. Evidently, I was supposed to put the greatest distance between the van and me by moving to the far side of the sidewalk so that it would not be easy for someone to leap out of the van and drag me into it. And I was apparently putting myself in danger whenever I parked my car beside a van in a parking lot for the same reason. I was also supposed to notice when I came back to the car, it seems, if a newly parked van was beside it. Vans seemed to figure largely in abductions, and the distinction between vans and friendly SUVs, full of children and harried mothers, had barely registered with me. Live and learn.

I decided that to keep myself really safe, I ought to go to a school for spies where I could get some intensive training. I'm not sure anything else would condition me to be constantly checking my surroundings and looking in store windows in case I could see the reflection of a man who may be stalking me.

There was more, of course, and I was pleased to note that I was alert to most dangers, especially at night. I avoided walking alone, was watchful when passing near alleys or darkened streets, crossed the street to avoid men singly or in groups, parked near entrances of buildings at night, and asked for help loading my car when grocery shopping after dark—a service most stores offered. In fact, after reading the first chapters, I realized I was actually very safety conscious. I had lived alone for a long time, and was the major caregiver for my young sister when I was still young myself, and I suppose I had absorbed safety information wherever it was offered. There must have been a lot of it and society had done a reasonably good job with me; although, my failure to watch out for parked vans and stalkers must mean that someone had fallen down on the job at some point.

That was enough for the night, I decided, and turned off the light, proud of myself for smoking only one cigarette that day. Maybe it was the thrill of knowing I could sleep in until seven-thirty or eight o'clock in the morning that had made me strong. With resolve like this, I could conquer the world.

-9-

Josh and I amused ourselves the next day with a variety of activities and non-stop talking, mostly guided by Josh. The district museum, our first stop, was a big hit with both of us. It is situated above the beautiful inner harbor in downtown Nanaimo, and our visit consumed the entire morning. We divided our time between the First Nation's exhibition with its stone arrowheads and other artifacts, and the next floor featuring the early days of Nanaimo. There was a replica of a coal mine and an authentic miner's cottage that commanded much of our attention, but Josh's favorite exhibit was the miniature reproduction of the old town of Nanaimo, encased in glass, where he could push a button on the wall and make an electric train travel through the town. The train obligingly stopped at the train station, the water tower, and other sites of interest. It traveled its circuit with Josh's help many times before I was able to lure him away to look at old toys from the early part of the century.

Hunger finally drove us out of the museum, and we had a fast-food lunch—Josh's choice—before finding a park and sharing a bit of fun on the playground equipment. I was glad there weren't too many children around so that I could have a turn on the swings. I managed to talk Josh out of trying to give me an "under-duck," although he was probably capable of giving me a good push and running under the swing as he did so, but I had visions of kicking him in the head and decided that might put a damper on our outing.

We returned home and made a collage of the leaves, feathers, and other odds and ends that Josh collected on our travels. The knowledge that Jody's funeral was being held today came to mind on only two or three occasions, and Josh managed to distract me each time.

That night, Josh and I washed and dried the dishes, tidied the living room, and put away his toys and the craft materials we had used. Under his watchful eye, I posted his artwork on the refrigerator door "to surprise Mommy," who would have been much more surprised if we hadn't produced a new craft for her to admire. I read him a story and tucked him into bed an hour later than his usual bedtime. Before I turned out the light, I asked him to tell me the best part of his day.

"Having you here was the best part of my day, Aunt Rachel," he said. The kid will go far.

I retired to the living room and picked up my half-finished book with a sigh. The best part of my day had been that I didn't have a moment to think about murders, suspects, and danger, and now, here I was, immersing myself in the subject again. I reminded myself this project was going to give Mandy some peace of mind, which made it worth doing. Personally, I didn't want to become paranoid regarding vans and stalkers.

I was hoping that the last half of the book would not involve do-it-yourself kung fu or karate lessons that I was expected to master by studying helpful diagrams but, no fear; what I found were basic yoga breathing techniques. The author claimed that all the victims of crime who had come to him for therapy had been too paralyzed with terror during their ordeal to make any real effort to save themselves when confronted by an attacker. His advice was to practice deep breathing techniques that could be used to keep yourself calm enough to seize any opportunity to escape, to scream, or to fight back any way that you could. He claimed that doing nothing would never save you from being raped, or beaten, or both, and doing something might—it might save you from being killed or might give you a chance to escape or be rescued. He urged his readers to practice the techniques daily.

I had practiced yoga off and on for years and the breathing exercises were very familiar. I wondered if I should review the techniques I had learned many years ago. Did I really need this? I squirmed uncomfortably as I considered my inability to deal with something as simple as a harmless spider dropping on me. I had been so upset at the restaurant, the simple solution of bending down to make the spider land on the floor and then step on it didn't even occur to me. What would I do if I came face-to-face with a really dangerous situation? Who was I kidding? I would panic, of course, and be incapable of rational thinking. There was no question—I had issues to address.

I was still reading when Mandy let herself into the house, tired but pleased with the success of her trip. I poured us each a glass of wine and we recounted the events of the day for each other. After Mandy finished her wine and slipped off to bed, I went back to my book, and managed to finish it before midnight. Should I go back to doing yoga every night to be on the safe side? After a brief consideration, I resolved to begin at once. I could even practice yoga at work whenever I received anything like the Chamber of Commerce article that had reared its ugly head on Thursday. Doing deep breathing exercises while standing on my head in the corner of the office would serve notice to everyone that I wasn't to be trifled with.

With that comforting scenario in mind, I called it a night.

The next morning, Mandy and I worked together in the kitchen to produce a huge brunch, and happy Josh pounced on the apple puff pancake and wolfed down half of it. I picked up the recipe from you-know-where, and, fortunately, it's a relatively healthy breakfast treat.

The day was cloudy, but the rain held off while we went outside to play some of Josh's favorite games on the lawn. When I reluctantly announced that it was time for me to head back to Victoria, we trooped indoors while I packed my few things, and I remembered to ask Mandy for the address of the Inn where she had seen Jody and Karl.

"I'm leaving the book here, Mandy," I said when I was ready to leave. "I finished it last night and you'll enjoy reading it, too. Thank you for buying it with me in mind, and you were right; there was useful information in it."

Mandy smiled. "I'm so glad. I was afraid to mention it in case you hated it."

"Oh, no. I enjoyed it."

There were hugs and kisses and thank you's all around, and I promised to come back for another visit soon. We waved our sad farewells as I pulled out of the driveway, and I was on my way.

The trip home was uneventful, and I almost enjoyed the drive. Not a black van to be seen anywhere.

❁ ❁ ❁

I let myself into my apartment with a sigh of relief. I hated to admit it, but Josh could both out-play and out-talk me, and I felt weary. I glanced at my carpet and decided that I didn't need to vacuum, and I had already changed the linens and washed my clothes before the weekend. I also had the forethought to stop and pick up a few groceries at the first available store when I drove into Victoria and had grabbed an early dinner at a drive-through restaurant. Let's see—after I unpacked my overnight bag and put away the groceries, were any other chores demanding my attention before the weekend drew to a close? No, there didn't seem to be. I could allow myself to sink into a stupor in front of the TV for the entire evening if I wanted to. In fact, the idea sounded great.

But first, I should make my call to the authorities. I fished around in my backpack for the number I had been given by the police in case I "thought of anything more that might help," and was very happy when the card surfaced without my being forced to empty the entire contents of the bag. I called the number and found myself talking to Constable "Szbbghgixhdk" at the "Pdjsdden" desk and was pleased to have identified two of the words he mumbled. I politely asked for a message to be given to Inspector Mitch Williams that I had some information for him. Well, why not? Mitch would certainly remember me and might loosen up and tell me something about how the investigation was going if I handed over a useful tip. Constable "Szbbghgixhdk" took my name and number and muttered something that sounded vaguely like "tanksavaniceday." I considered replying, "Easy for you to say," but I didn't need any enemies on the force, and contented myself with a simple "thank you."

When I was finally free to collapse on the sofa and begin channel surfing, my chance to relax didn't last for long. The phone rang a minute or two after I had myself nicely settled, and I groaned as I heaved myself to my feet. Who would be calling me at an hour usually reserved for dinner? I prepared to deliver my usual cold-hearted response to a phone solicitation, but instead learned that my caller was none other than Inspector Williams.

"I understand you have some information for me," he said, "and I'm in your neighborhood. Why don't I drop by? Will that be convenient?"

"Sure," I answered, surprised. I was going to tell him my address, but before I could say another word, I heard, "Okay, I'll be there in ten minutes," and he hung up.

So, he consulted a notebook where he has my address listed with those of all the other suspects in the case? Or had Inspector Williams received my message and asked Constable Szbbghgixhdk to look up my address in the records and then forced him to slow down and enunciate when he passed along the information?

I took a bottle of Chardonnay out of the fridge and a bottle of Chianti out of the cupboard and put them on the counter along with two wineglasses. This time I would remember to ask whether my guest preferred red or white wine—unless, of course, he considered himself on duty and wouldn't drink any alcohol. I looked at the coffeepot and decided not to bother with coffee unless the wine was refused. I also pulled my notebook out of my handbag and found the page where I had written the name of the Inn and the address and phone number for it, copied from the card Mandy had provided.

I was ready—except for running a brush through my hair, I suddenly remembered, and hurried into the bathroom to perform that task. I also inspected my teeth for food bits that might be clinging to them after my hasty, fast-food dinner, and put on some more lipstick. It had not slipped my mind that he was a handsome devil.

My phone gave two short rings, indicating someone at the entrance for me, and, when I picked it up, my caller identified himself as "Mitch," not "Inspector Williams." I pressed the number on the phone that would release the front door and didn't try to tell him how to find my apartment or its number. I'm a fast learner.

He smiled when I answered the door and automatically ducked his head when he entered the room in spite of its eight-foot ceiling. There are probably scars under that thick hair from wounds inflicted before he learned not to take the height of doorways and ceilings for granted. He was bearing two cardboard cups of coffee and he handed one to me.

"Thank you," I said, surprised. "I was going to offer you wine, but coffee is great. Let me pour it into a couple of mugs." He followed me to the kitchen and examined the Chianti bottle while I pulled two of my largest mugs out of the cupboard and carefully emptied the contents of the cardboard containers into them.

"I'm glad I brought the coffee. It makes it easier to turn down a glass of Chianti; I'm still on duty," he explained with a regretful sigh, as he picked up one of the mugs. We went into the living room and he took a seat in the recliner, generously offered by his hostess.

"So, what have you got for me?" Mitch asked after I, clutching my notebook, seated myself across from him on the sofa and we had both taken sips of coffee.

"An address," I said, and waited for him to pull out his notebook, which he did. I read it out, and he copied it down. He didn't ask, just looked up expectantly.

"Apparently, Jody Smythe and Karl Ullman were friends. Maybe more than that. My sister, Mandy, and her friend saw them at that Inn near Parksville eating dinner together a couple of weeks ago. Their impression was—to use my sister's words—they were more than good friends."

"Well, well, well," said Mitch softly, "could be important. Karl denied knowing Jody."

I was pleased that he told me that much and decided to go for broke. "Did the autopsy show that the killer was standing behind Jody and was the murder weapon really a knife?"

"Yes, to both questions, although we haven't found the knife yet."

Good. He was cracking under the influence of his coffee and my carefully combed hair. "How about the autopsy on Kevin? Was he killed before or after Jody, and was a knife used on him, too?"

Mitch stared at me without speaking for a moment. Finally, he said, "I don't suppose there is any harm in telling you. He was killed a few hours before Jody, and, yes, it was with a knife. We believe it was the same knife, and it's either a butcher knife or something very similar. There is an interesting difference between the two wounds—there were soil particles found in Jody's wound."

I worked that one out. "Soil? So, the knife was stuck in the ground, or dropped on the ground, or wiped on the ground between the time Kevin was killed and Jody was killed."

"That's right. It was definitely fresh soil. Pity it isn't some distinctive soil that we could identify as belonging to a particular garden in Victoria, but no such luck."

"So, you believe the murders are connected."

"It's very probable; we're assuming they probably are."

"You won't really know unless you catch him—or her."

"Oh, we'll catch whoever it is sooner or later."

"I guessed you were trying to find some connection between the two," I said. "The mall where Kevin's van was found isn't that far from the Ullman Building—walking distance, in fact."

I settled back into my chair, more comfortable now that I had performed my civic duty. "I reminded Audrey Renwick when I saw her again that she originally told me she saw a Hasty Xpress courier entering the building at lunch time on Monday. But she wouldn't admit it. I knew there was a possibility that she wanted to avoid going on record in a statement to the police, but she wouldn't confirm that either."

"It's one of the occupational hazards of police work," said Mitch. "We get a lot of witnesses who suddenly forget every important observation they initially made. Mind you, we also get people who suddenly remember key observations that they couldn't possibly have made." He laughed shortly and shook his head.

However, I was off on my own train of thought and didn't bother to offer any comforting words. "So, it probably means Jody knew something regarding Kevin's murder, or Kevin knew the reason, or a possible reason, that Jody was murdered. Or maybe the murderer needed a disguise to get into the building."

I sat pondering the problem for a moment and then looked up to see Mitch watching me. "Did you find his Hasty X cap yet? And did you find his clipboard?" I asked.

He shook his head and appeared to be waiting for more. I obliged. "Have you considered a drug angle or blackmail, perhaps?"

"We always look at financial dealings whenever a murder occurs," he said, "and there doesn't appear to be any involvement with drugs that we can find. Neither of the two victims were users, there have been no reports of drugs disappearing from Evergreen Manor, and Jody wasn't wealthy or, at least, doesn't appear to be. We haven't uncovered any bank accounts suggesting income other than what she earned at The Manor and from her modest investments, which also rules out blackmail and many other illicit activities. Kevin was young with a young family and lived as you might expect—a big mortgage on a small house; a modest car; a wife planning to go back to work in another year or two. We're still lacking motive."

"I wasn't told anything about Jody's family. I know the funeral was held in Vancouver today, and I understand her mother lives there."

Mitch nodded. "Yes, we attended the funeral, of course, and a number of people from Evergreen Manor were there, too, but the majority of mourners were friends of the mother and well on in years. There are no other relatives, and Jody lived in Victoria for most of her adult life and kept to herself, it seems. Although, not as much as we thought, perhaps," he added, looking down at his notebook.

"Is there money in the family that she stood to inherit?"

Mitch shook his head.

"People tell me she was a very nice person and everyone liked her," I said, wondering if he would tell me any of her dark secrets if the police knew any.

"Yes, we've been told the same thing." He smiled faintly. "Mind you we often hear that kind of remark from people at first and it doesn't always turn out to be true. However, Jody really does seem to have been well liked by almost everyone, or so they say."

I couldn't think of anything more to ask him, nor did Mitch have anything more to ask me, apparently. He finished his coffee, put down the mug, and stood up, but didn't race to the door. Instead, he walked over to one of the bookcases where some photos of Mandy at various ages were displayed, thereby giving me an opportunity to check him out without having to watch where my eyes strayed.

"Is this your sister?" he asked after studying the photos for a while.

"Yes, that's Amanda, or Mandy, as she is usually called, and that's a picture of her son, my nephew, Josh, on the other shelf."

He smiled. "She's pretty, and Josh is a good-looking boy, too. But that doesn't surprise me," he added without looking at me.

I was astonished, but before I had a chance to dream up a response, he said, "I understand you lost your husband in a car accident. I'm sorry."

"Thank you," I said, happy that my reply covered both remarks, and I followed him as he turned and walked to the door. With his hand on the doorknob, he looked down at me. "I appreciate the information you gave me but, look, don't go asking questions of the people in and around your building, okay? Thank you for trying to find out whether Ms. Renwick would remember seeing a Hasty Xpress courier because it was you asking rather than the police, but don't do anything like that again. You never know who might be dangerous, and how close he might be. You've given us useful information, and it is always good for us to get an outside perspective on events, but remember, you gave me information about a man that you know who owns, and is often in, your building. Until we check it out, and until we find out who was responsible for these killings, walk softly."

"And carry a big stick," I finished the quote, while registering the fact that he wasn't wearing a wedding ring.

"A stick doesn't provide much protection against a knife," he said seriously as he opened the door and stepped out into the hall. "Take care."

"Good night," I replied.

Yes! I had picked up quite a bit from that little visit and the man must like me if that left-handed compliment was anything to go on and I went back to the TV feeling elated. My evening, short though it was and with Monday morning looming all too soon, passed in a pleasant glow of satisfaction. In fact, I almost forgot to practice my yoga breathing, but remembered when I was brushing my teeth before going to bed. I virtuously marched back into the living room, lit a candle, and sat down on the floor in my nightgown. When I arose about fifteen minutes later, my lungs well exercised, I felt a bit sleepy and pleasantly relaxed. Yes, I would be in great shape to deal with any future crisis as long as my deep breathing didn't cause me to fall asleep in the middle of it.

-10-

I relayed the events of the weekend to Donna the next morning and told her what I had learned about Karl and passed along to Mitch. She was suitably impressed and delighted.

"I knew it! I knew it! Karl did it!" she chortled.

"Not so fast. It's entirely possible Jody and Karl ran into each other somewhere and decided to have dinner together. Mandy and her friend Heather thought there was more to it than that, but they don't know it for a fact. We have to wait until the police check it out."

"Mandy is pretty sharp. If she thinks it was an intimate dinner, you may be sure it was. And I wouldn't put anything past that Karl," Donna said. "I wonder how long it will take the police to 'make their inquiries.'"

We didn't have long to wait. A few minutes before lunch, Cyndi came to us with the information that Karl had been taken to the police station for questioning. The story was reported on the eleven o'clock news she told us, and people all over the building were talking about it.

"Bless us all here, the police made the trip up Island and back in record time," Donna said after Cyndi left the room having expressed shock that a nice man like Karl could be a suspect in the case simply because he happened to have been in the Ullman Building that day—which filled in another piece of the puzzle.

"Maybe not. They might have asked the police Up Island to check it out for them, or perhaps they didn't bother," I replied mildly. "They don't have to establish what kind of relationship Jody and Karl had—only that they were acquainted with each other. Mitch told me that Karl said he hadn't met her, which he obviously had, and that's reason enough for the police to want to take a closer look at him. They didn't even have to find out for sure. They could have told him they learned about the two of them, and, if it were true, Karl probably wouldn't bother to deny it or ask who told them that. And he was here that day, as Cyndi mentioned. He must have walked over here from his other office as you suggested."

"I wonder what Karl's wife will think about this. Her husband was not only having an affair; he's now a suspect in a murder case," said Donna jumping to conclusions all over the place.

"Maybe she knows Karl and Jody were having an affair and she killed Jody," I offered, giving up any hope of curbing Donna's imagination. "And she killed Kevin because he's the one who told her about it the night they met at a dinner party. She stole Kevin's Hasty X cap as a souvenir and has hidden it in her bottom drawer under her lingerie."

Donna looked at me in exasperation.

"Well, you told me that your Sean could come up with a better story than I could," I said defensively. "My reputation for fiction is at stake. Anyway, the situation would supply Karl's wife with a motive but I don't see that Karl has one. Maybe his wife loves him."

"Nobody could love Karl," Donna snorted. "Besides, I met his wife and I like her."

"That would be her defense, of course. I'm innocent; ask Donna O'Hare how nice I am."

"I think it's more likely that Karl made an indecent proposal to Jody, and she turned him down flat and threatened to tell his wife, and so he killed her," Donna said reflectively. "That makes more sense. And Kevin saw Jody and Karl together and he had to be put out of the way, too."

"Right. That must be it. But makes you wonder why Karl didn't go after the people who had dinner at the Inn the night he and Jody were there. And the waiters, too, and anybody else who ever saw them together. In fact, it doesn't sound to me as though Karl covered himself with glory by killing off Jody and Kevin. His work had only begun. What is he waiting for? And why did Jody come over to our building if the police can make a case out of that one? Did Karl invite the woman who had spurned him to come over for a little chat? And she came? I don't think so. Which reminds me—how many indecent proposals of Karl's have you rejected and are alive to talk about?"

"Okay, okay, but are you seriously suggesting that your stupid explanation could be the right one?"

"No, but there must be something more to it than an affair between a single woman and a married man to have two people wind up dead. A third of the adult population would have been killed off by now."

"What do you think happened?"

"I think we should consider the possibility that there are drugs or money or a blackmail threat involved, and I think Kevin was murdered because his cap and his clipboard offered a way for the killer to get into the building. Maybe there was no plan to kill him initially, but Kevin ran into a man taking those things from his van, and he could now identify him. That knowledge made Kevin dangerous. Couriers aren't noticed in buildings except by the people talking to them because couriers *belong*. Audrey didn't look at whoever it was. Or, at least, she says she didn't."

"Okay, I can see Karl as a drug lord. He was buying drugs from Jody. She was coming over to tell him that her conscience was bothering her, and the supply would be cut off. Oh, yes, and she was going to the authorities to confess. Or else she owed him money and couldn't pay. How's that?"

"If she were supplying drugs from The Manor, then Karl was the buyer and he would be the one owing money, not her. Besides, her body was facing up the stairs, and her killer was behind her. If Karl were in the building and she went upstairs to his office with the news that she would no longer supply him with drugs and was going to confess her crime, he would have had to follow her down the stairs afterwards, and she would have been found facing down the stairs not up. And who was the courier and why was he in the building at the same time? And why was Kevin killed?"

"You're a pain in the ass, you are. We zeroed in on Karl as the killer right away, and you've now forgotten our brilliant deductive reasoning," Donna said.

"You're right, I have. Why not give me a recap of our brilliant deductive reasoning that led us to suspect Karl right away. What was it again? Something about his being a jerk and our not liking him?"

Maybe it's just as well that the phone rang for Donna at that point and once she was engaged, I returned to the draft of my article on Stuart's actuarial consulting business. It was time we got some work done around here.

❀ ❀ ❀

After an uninspiring bag lunch, I trudged over to The Manor for my interview with Katherine Parker, taking the route by the road out of respect for my high heels donned for the occasion. I had taken care with my wardrobe in honor of this interview today and was snappily dressed in a suit and tailored blouse. It's good to remind people now and then that I actually own and wear something other than slacks and jeans.

I was interested in my first glimpse of the woman described to me by so many people but on whom I had never laid eyes, as far as I knew. I was not disappointed. Katherine was in her mid-sixties, trim and elegant looking. Her carefully waved white hair was still thick, and she wore contemporary dark-rimmed glasses, behind which were a pair of very observant brown eyes. She wore discreet makeup and a diamond pin and earrings, two rings with diamond clusters and a number of gold bands. She was dressed in a well-cut mauve suit with matching high heels, and a white tailored blouse. The effect didn't scream money; it stated it calmly using the finest cultured diction.

Katherine welcomed me graciously into the office and I nodded to a pleasant-looking woman who was manning the phone and could not be introduced. She appeared to be roughly the same age as Katherine, and I concluded that this must be Marianne of the Guy and Marianne team. Marianne was thin, with gray hair pulled into a loose coil at the back of her neck and fastened with a tortoise-shell comb. Unlike Katherine, her clothes were unremarkable, and she was sensibly shod; however, she looked up from the phone to give me a wide, friendly smile as Katherine whisked me into the inner office.

The interview went easily, and Katherine was enthusiastic and obviously proud of the seniors' residence she owned. After she answered the questions I had prepared, she took me on a tour of the facilities, which ended downstairs in a large room with a fireplace, overstuffed sofas, and an extremely large television set and a DVD player. She explained that every Friday night was movie night, complete with popcorn, and the event was popular with the residents. Sliding glass doors along one wall led outside to a brick patio, and, beyond it were the beautiful, well-kept gardens. We could see into a small adjoining room that could seat twelve people around four card tables, and there were a variety of board games and decks of cards displayed on open shelves. Katherine looked around approvingly at the half-dozen, or so, seniors chatting companionably or playing cards in these two rooms. "I want the residents to feel the apartments are their homes as individuals, and the shared areas are their homes as a community," she said grandly, spreading her arms wide as though to gather up all the residents and hold them to her heart.

Corny, of course, but it would make good copy, and what's more, it was very likely true. The residents seemed to be enjoying themselves hugely at Evergreen Manor—happy, involved, and entertained. They had privacy as well as companionship, and help was available when they needed it. More information about the business side of running the residence would come from David, but I had enough information to write about the lifestyle one could expect for the prices charged. As well, I understood something about the commitment it took from the owner and managers to maintain the services that made this facility so attractive.

I was lavish in my praise of what I had seen at The Manor, and it was genuine. I also made sure Katherine realized that I had a couple of friends in the residence in case she saw me there now and then in the near future. I wanted to do a little more probing about David in case he started dating my friend before a jury returned a guilty verdict for someone else in the Jody and Kevin cases. In addition, if drugs were disappearing from The Manor, sooner or later someone would let a comment slip, and I wanted to be there to catch it. I took advantage of the moment to ask innocently, "Was arranging tours for the seniors and looking after the movie night the kind of thing poor Jody used to do?"

Katherine was probably annoyed that I had brought up the very name she had been avoiding whenever she mentioned the activities and responsibilities of the managers, but she handled it well. "Exactly," and she sighed dramatically. "The residents miss her so much; it will be hard to replace her."

"Did you notice the large grill we have outside on the patio," she swept on, without missing a beat. "We serve barbecue lunches in addition to our regular lunch for those who like to eat outside when the weather is fine."

"How nice. And I understand that a number of residents joined you at the funeral on Saturday," I said. "I'm sure Jody's mother was happy about that. But I guess both you and David feel as though you have lost a friend as well as a co-worker."

Katherine hesitated a moment, but probably realized that I would know David had been held by the police for questioning early in the game. She certainly wouldn't want to create the impression that David and Jody were not good friends, but how truthful would she be?

"Jody was a fine person," she said primly, "and David thought so, too. Jody probably believed she was closer to David than she was, of course. He is charming to everyone, and sometimes that can be misinterpreted. He has a lot of common sense and isn't easily fooled."

So, Jody chased after David, but David wasn't having any, simply because he had too much sense to fall for a girl who wasn't all she appeared to be—whatever that might mean. At least, that's the story from Katherine. How far would Katherine go to ensure that she could keep her charming son to herself? I tried to imagine the elegant Katherine murdering someone and almost laughed.

"The police were here trying to find out if Jody and that courier person who was killed were friends, or something. I certainly gave them a piece of my mind. We never use Hasty Xpress couriers, and I wouldn't have kept a female employee who would date a married man."

I jumped in. "Kevin Lewis was *our* courier; he came to our office almost every day. I don't imagine the police believe that Jody and Kevin were necessarily dating. It is likely just a matter of finding out if the two of them knew each other and if they both knew someone who might have a motive to kill one or both of them."

"Yes, of course." Katherine had recovered and gracefully skirted the issue. "Such a sorrow for the poor young man's family. I have a nephew in Vancouver who is a courier for Hasty Xpress."

I wasn't sure what conclusion I was supposed to draw from that comment, but decided she was probably trying to say that couriers were nice people who didn't deserve to be murdered. It was obviously time to thank her for the interview and get myself out of there. We said nice things to each other, and I left her downstairs chatting with a couple of elderly men who seemed pleased by her attention.

Upstairs and on my way to the front door, I caught sight of Mrs. T sitting by herself in the dining room. I immediately changed direction and made a beeline for her.

"How are you today?" I asked as I pulled a chair up to her table. "And where is Seatie this afternoon?" as a memory jog, in case she couldn't remember where she had seen me before.

"I'm fine," Mrs. T answered easily enough, "and Seatie will be along in a moment. She went to get a sweater." She nodded towards a teacup in use, indicating that it was Seatie's and only temporarily abandoned.

I went straight to the point. "I was talking to Katherine a few moments ago, and she suggested that Jody was more interested in David than David was in Jody." I settled back to see how that would fly.

Mrs. T didn't answer at once and seemed to be turning the idea over. "That could be," she finally answered, "but Katherine wouldn't know that for sure, and would assume the worst, just in case."

"Why?" I asked.

Mrs. T shrugged. "Some women are like that about their sons. Can't bear to share them. She stopped David from marrying once before, I remember, but he was much younger then. Probably didn't understand what was happening until it was too late. However, David and his mother get along well, and he's good to her."

Meaning all was forgiven, and he understood? I wondered if being good to his mother included staying a bachelor for the rest of his life to make her happy, but I couldn't find the words to ask that. In any case, Seatie was slowly making her way to the table with a radiant smile. Too late.

However, after Seatie and I had greeted each other, Mrs. T continued talking, as though there had been no interruption. "The police searched the kitchen for a knife, you know."

Seatie looked startled at this news flash, but quickly explained, "Mrs. T is talking about the time that David was taken to the police station. Officers came in and looked through the kitchen that day and we heard they were examining the knives. Such nonsense and so upsetting for everyone."

"The cook wasn't upset, but Guy was," Mrs. T went on. And then, out of the blue, "Guy and Marianne don't get along." She pointed to a man passing through the main room, dressed in what looked like a chauffeur's uniform.

Now it was my turn to be startled. Not only that, I felt as though I had been dumped without warning onto a rollercoaster. I was having trouble following Mrs. T's abrupt changes of direction. "That's Marianne's husband?" He looked to be in his late fifties, which would probably make him younger than the woman I had seen on the phone in the office, and he was nice looking.

"Yes, that's him. He's dressed to take a group out in the van for their appointments. He has quite an eye for the ladies. And he's younger than Marianne, too."

"Now, dear, we mustn't gossip," Seatie interjected, "And, of course, he *is* a Frenchman," she added, as though that explained everything. Obviously uncomfortable, she quickly changed the subject: "Would you like a cup of coffee? How remiss of us not to have offered sooner."

I declined with thanks and took my leave with the excuse of having to return to the office and get some work done, and truer words were never spoken. I hurried down the garden path and picked my way through the shrubs to take the shortcut—high heels not withstanding—through the large treed lot separating The Manor from the Ullman Building.

Once I was deep into the trees and brush, it was astonishingly quiet. There were buildings, parking lots, and streets surrounding the property, but it was hard to believe when the snapping of twigs underfoot was the only noise I could identify. I soon realized I could hear other things as well—the sound of crickets grew louder and louder and the squirrels and chipmunks were making little squirrel and chipmunk noises, and some bird nearby was singing loudly. My heels sunk into the soft ground every few paces and whatever time I thought I was going to save by taking this shortcut was rapidly disappearing.

I wondered if I were retracing the route taken by Jody or her killer or both, and I looked around uneasily I as dodged the lower hanging branches and kept a sharp eye out for spider webs. Just as I began considering going back and taking the road to spare my shoes any further grief, the trees opened up and I could see the top of the Ullman building straight ahead.

I heaved a sigh of relief, walked to the edge of the lot, and paused to scrape the mud off my shoes. I lit a cigarette before I stepped out of the bush and onto the pavement of the Ullman parking lot. I was already later than I should have been but I was stressed.

What I had learned from Mrs. T was certainly more interesting than anything Katherine told me, even if I couldn't use the material in my article. Mrs. T seemed to know everything that was going on around the place and the fact that she wasn't the soul of tact was all to the good, although it took some effort to follow her staccato delivery of information.

I decided it might be worthwhile talking to Marianne, and although it wasn't part of our interview arrangements for the article, I could justify it easily enough. I would simply invent questions for her and then express my sympathy about Jody and how not having a replacement for her must be causing a lot of extra work for the staff, etcetera. If Guy had a thing for Jody, Marianne would probably be aware of it and would not be mourning Jody's loss to any great extent. I could likely spot the lack of warmth and take my lead from there. In addition, if residents complained about drugs disappearing from their rooms, Marianne would surely know about it and would be more likely to admit it to a sympathetic listener than to the police. If she thought there were any chance that a woman who might have been a threat to her marriage had been involved, she might indicate that, too. Katherine, on the other hand, would be very dodgy about admitting to anything that might cast a reflection on the safety of the residents and would certainly take pains to hide such information if at all possible. I could see her brushing aside any complaints from the residents, and sympathetically and urgently convincing them that they had forgotten how many pills they had left in a bottle or that they must have inadvertently tossed out a bottle that wasn't empty. Marianne, however, was probably more objective and might be more interested in finding out the truth.

What did I have here? Karl involved with Jody? Guy and Jody romantically involved? David and Jody? Did Karl win Jody's attention and drive Guy into a murderous rage? Or was it David? Or could it have been Marianne? Maybe this was a run-of-the mill, classic love triangle.

I sighed and realized that I had more questions than answers after my visits to The Manor. Jody certainly wasn't as particular about choosing only unmarried male "friends" as Seatie had assumed, but would that make her a target for murder in these days of casual sex and easy divorce? In any case, I had heard nothing that would clear David from being involved in either sex or drugs or, for that matter, rock-and-roll.

I emerged onto the Ullman property, ground out the remains of my cigarette on the pavement, and walked around to the front entrance. I didn't even glance at the side door which I hadn't used since that awful Monday. I would take a book by Rinehart to The Manor tomorrow and lend it to Seatie as an excuse for another visit. I could persuade her to introduce me to Marianne if I asked, and Seatie would have no suspicion that I had any ulterior motive. Mrs. T, of course, was another matter altogether, and I had a feeling that she could see right through me. I had better watch my step there.

Cyndi was pleased when she heard that I had visited Seatie again and scolded herself for neglecting her old friend. I told her that Seatie was fine and so was Mrs. T, Seatie's friend. Cyndi dismissed Mrs. T with a wave of her hand. "I know Seatie spends time with Mrs. T because she feels sorry for her. Mrs. T makes things up and no one believes a word she says. She's so silly. She's probably becoming senile, even though she isn't nearly as old as Seatie."

I digested this idea as I made my way to the back office. Could that be true? Seatie often tried to stop Mrs. T from saying things that were, perhaps, in poor taste, but she never actually contradicted anything Mrs. T said. So, did Mrs. T really make up stories and, if not, who had suggested such a thing to Cyndi? Interesting.

But, of course, when I started working, the question wasn't interesting enough to distract me as I wrestled with the problem of trying to fit a great long story about a wonderful service for our readers into a four by four inch ad. Especially as I had to include, somehow, the company logo and a photograph of the provider of the service, as well. I looked with loathing at the advertiser's grinning face while I struggled with the problem for a good part of an hour. Donna, immersed in her bookkeeping duties for most of the day and trying to decide which bills required her immediate and urgent attention, was incapable of giving me the sympathy I deserved.

When I finally pulled off an ad design miracle and started working on the next ad in my file, I looked with dismay at the collection of ads that still remained. I didn't even want to open my editing file. I really needed to stay late for a few nights so that I could get these ads out of the way. Donna and I had agreed long ago that I would never take work home with me since, because of the nature of her work, she would never have to do that. So, the company didn't buy me a home computer, and, without one, I really couldn't work at home.

"Take work home, and pretty soon it becomes a habit," Donna had said forcefully when we were setting up the business and working out the division of labor. "Before you know it, you'll be working many more hours than I will and, in time, you'll feel resentful and I'll feel guilty. It would ruin everything. This job will only be fun if we are doing it together. Promise me that no matter how tight our schedules become, you will never take work home."

Well, I had promised, but, of course, I often work late at the office when our printing deadline approaches. Donna accepts this as a necessary evil, never fails to ask me how many hours I've worked, and keeps a scrupulous record. She always knows exactly how many hours or days I should take off when we start on the next production cycle, and demands that I do so. Unfortunately, we hadn't foreseen a situation that would make it awkward for me to stay late at the office, and we are going to have to work something out.

The three of us closed up shop at five o'clock and left together, but my unfinished workload lay heavy on my mind as I drove unhappily back to my apartment. I cheered up somewhat when I caught sight of Ryan on his way out of the apartment building as I drove up. He saw me and stopped, waiting expectantly. It was my turn to add a couplet to the *Adventures of Ned* and I was ready. I called out the last two lines as I approached him, along with my addition:

"His mouth dissolving in a pout

He shuddered as he fished it out."

I then added: "'Tis such that causes my despair,

And he dried the joint on his long, blond hair."

Ryan nodded, smiled, and gave me a wave before he walked on. I love to have an appreciative audience.

-11-

Tuesday did not start well. I had a restless sleep and morning came much too soon. I dragged myself to the office unhappily, remembering that it was only one week and one day since two people we knew had been murdered, and felt even more unhappy when I found Donna preparing to go out and pick up what she announced was the last of the ads.

"The last of the ads?" I wailed as I made my way to my desk, holding my cardboard coffee cup in front of me like a holy crucifix warding off the devil. "I thought we had all of them. Tell me the last of the ads are camera-ready and all I have to do is scan them into the computer."

"No such luck," said Donna, with unnecessary cheerfulness. "Anyway, there are only four more. I told you there were a few coming in late. It's all money in our pockets."

"I'll never catch up; I'm so far …" and that's when I walked straight into my hanging plant, banging my head, and dumping a half cup of cardboard-tasting coffee all over the floor, my shoes, and the bottom of my slacks.

Donna, exclaimed, "Oh, no, are you all right?" and then spoiled the effect by adding, "Watch out for the spider ... ha, ha, ha ... plant!" She was pulling handfuls of tissues out of a box and helpfully dabbing at my slacks while trying to muffle her tittering, but that hardly made up for it. I plunked myself down behind my desk and told her to get out before she found herself dangling at the end of Cyndi's decorative chain. Donna, still not able to spit out an intelligible sentence, picked up her briefcase, gave me an apologetic wave and left.

I sighed, grabbed a few paper towels and mopped up the floor, swiped at my shoes, and inspected my slacks. They were already drying, and the coffee splashes didn't seem to be noticeable; and the pain in my head was also fading fast. There was one swallow of coffee left in the container, and so I downed it. There was no reason not to get to work right away and so I opened my computer and got to it. About twenty minutes later when I was putting the finishing touches to the article about Stuart's consulting firm, I paused and the whole scene flashed to mind. I suddenly saw myself, Super Klutz, walking into the hanging plant, and broke up, giggling over my keyboard.

Cyndi walked into the office with the mail while I was in the midst of this private jocularity and looked a bit startled, but then smiled indulgently, and said, "I'm glad to see you are in such a good mood. Donna thought you were a bit worried about all the work piling up on you."

"No, everything's fine. I'll manage," I said, not wanting any reassurances about tomorrow being a brighter day, and the darkest hour coming before the dawn. I stared fixedly at the computer screen with unseeing eyes until she left and I was alone again, and then I sat there for a few minutes longer while I allowed myself to think about David. I was going to interview him tomorrow morning and would finally have a chance to form my own opinion about him. But how many times do we hear that criminals have great charisma, and would I be immune if David turned the full wattage of his charm on me? I would have to rely on picking up some evil thought-waves emanating from him. Would I be reassured if he turned out to be an ordinary, nice man, who just happened to look like a movie star? Probably not. I was going to have to continue with my own version of a background check, which meant relying on information gleaned from anywhere I could get it. I glanced over at my backpack in which the book by Mary Roberts Rinehart was tucked, my passport into The Manor and, with luck, culminating in an introduction to Marianne. I looked guiltily back at the work on my desk and wondered if I could take time for a trip to The Manor today. Maybe not.

I sighed. Donna had been falling in and out of love with unsuitable men since I had known her, and my role, until now, was only to help pick up the pieces when things fell apart. This situation, however, was different. We weren't talking about a bad relationship, but Donna's safety, and I wanted something concrete to tell her to bring her to her senses and forget pursuing this David character until his innocence in our recent spate of murders was firmly established. Was I up to the skillful questioning of The Hottie that might be required?

What would David say, for instance, if I told him that it was common knowledge that residents complained about prescription medicines disappearing from their rooms? He might deny it or he might ask me where I heard such a thing. It was useful to be in the writing-editing business at such times. I could fall back on that oft-repeated phrase—so irritating to the listener, I'm sure—"I have my sources." Of course, those words often meant, "I made the whole thing up to see if I could trap you into saying something damaging about yourself," and sometimes it actually worked.

I resolved to go over to The Manor after lunch no matter what my ad file looked like or at what stage my editing had stalled. It would be useful to learn as much as possible from my two new friends and possibly Marianne before I conducted my interview with David tomorrow morning. If Marianne appeared absolutely astonished at the idea of drugs disappearing from The Manor, and if her attitude also forced me to discard the notion that David had anything going on with Jody, I could relax a bit. The police had a little more experience in solving crimes than I had, and I could safely leave the whole thing to them—and I'm sure they would be thrilled to hear that. Perhaps I would call Inspector Mitch Williams and tell him the good news afterwards. I would finish constructing my ads, write my lead article, complete the bit of editing I had left to do, and live happily ever after. The police would solve their case, Donna and David might have a few dates which could lead to a good relationship or even a long-term relationship, or maybe not. It really wasn't any of my business.

I turned back to my computer in a happier frame of mind, but determined to slip over to The Manor and track Seatie down this afternoon like the super-sleuth that I am.

"Take a look at this," said Donna as she breezed into the office later in the morning, pulling out something frilly and frothy from the plastic bag tucked into her briefcase.

"Wonderful. Has one of our advertisers fallen for me?" I asked as I picked up the lace panties and matching bra. "Who sent them?"

"As if. The insurance office where I was picking up one of our ads is located right by a lingerie boutique. I bought these on sale in case I need them soon, I hope."

"Very pretty, and I wish you joy. Now let me see how much work you brought me."

"It's not too bad. All the ads are pretty straightforward and there is only one photo to deal with," she said as she tossed four envelopes on my desk. "I'm going to get my lunch from the fridge. I have to heat it. Are you going to stop for lunch now? Did you bring anything?"

"Yes. I have a salad and an apple, and I'm going to hit up Cyndi for a cup of tea. The microwave is all yours."

"Good. The stuff may not smell too great when I'm heating it, but it is guaranteed to work."

"The stuff?" I repeated, pretending to be mystified, although I had immediately guessed what was coming. "What stuff? And what do you mean by 'work'? Work to cure your hunger pangs? Work to give you the energy you need for this afternoon's labors? Work to boost your immune system?"

I was not surprised when she explained: "The 'stuff' is called 'miracle soup' and it's guaranteed to take five pounds off the first week, and I will lose three to five pounds every week after that. I eat it three times a day with vegetables on the first day, with fruit on the second day, with a mixture of fruit and vegetables on day three, and ...." She frowned in concentration. "I'll have to look at the sheet again to see what I eat with it for the rest of the week. My friend, Sharon, gave the diet to me. She's lost twenty pounds since she started it."

"How has she felt while all this weight loss has been going on? I'm working in close contact with you and have a vested interest in obstructing anything that destroys your sunny disposition."

"I'll be fine. Sharon said it was really easy to stay on this diet because the soup is so nutritious and tasty, and the meals aren't boring because you eat different things each day."

"Except for the soup, of course. Eating the same soup three times a day might be a bit monotonous. And what are the main ingredients of this tasty and nutritious dish, dare I ask?"

"Cabbage and tomatoes, and a bunch of other vegetables and spices."

"Sounds charming. Suddenly, my salad and apple sounds like a gourmet feast, but don't let me discourage you."

"You won't," Donna replied airily, as if the whole history of her inability to incorporate any eating restrictions into her diet for longer than three days had totally vanished from her mind.

We ate our lunch together while Cyndi slipped off to her health club for her exercise class. She had made no nasty comment about the odor of Donna's miracle soup as it heated up even though it was truly worthy of a nasty comment in my opinion, and Cyndi also kindly made us a pot of herbal tea before she left. Donna's new diet allowed her to drink all the herbal tea she wanted, and she gamely downed two cups—a measure of her commitment to losing weight. She normally made a great pretense of gagging at the thought of drinking herbal tea, but I didn't remind her of that, loyal and supportive friend that I am.

Once lunch was over, I took advantage of Donna's engrossment in a phone call to grab my backpack and leave, giving her a wave as I did so. She looked a bit surprised, but waved back, probably assuming I had an appointment she had forgotten about.

When I pushed open the front door of The Manor, the office to my right was empty. I did a quick scan of the people lingering over their luncheon beverages in the main room, hoping to find Seatie among them. I was about to head down the hall to her apartment when she called my name. I turned to see that she had separated herself from a group of ladies seated on the far side of the room and was slowly making her way through the maze of tables towards me with a welcoming smile. I dug into my backpack and pulled out the Rinehart murder mystery and held it aloft for her to see. Her smile broadened.

"My Dear, how sweet of you to remember. I have really been looking forward to reading a new author," she said, when she reached me. "Do come and sit for a while. Would you like some tea or coffee?"

I politely declined any refreshment, but was happy to join her at one of the tables within a few feet of the office. I could keep a sharp eye out for Marianne from this vantage point if she had office duties today. I passed the book over and was rewarded by an appreciative smile as Seatie examined the picture of a gun on the front cover with apparent relish. "You're so thoughtful. I'll take good care of it," she said.

"I hope you enjoy it," I said, pleased with myself.

There was a pause and then Seatie looked up at me a bit guiltily. "Do you know any details of the investigation into Jody's death? Or anything about the young man who died the same day?" she asked. Obviously, she had had some second thoughts about the victims being indiscriminately chosen by a released convict who killed with no apparent motive. "We heard that the police were questioning the landlord of your building, but, of course, he's a married man, and I can't imagine Jody having anything to do with a married man," she said, steadfastly sticking to her belief in Jody's moral rectitude. "Have you learned anything more?"

"Not much," I confessed, "but the investigation is still going on, and the police need time to put everything together. I imagine they'll be questioning a lot of people." I didn't want to tell her the gossip about Jody and Karl since it might not be true and Karl might be released at any time, just as David had been.

Seatie sighed. "I wish it were as easy as solving a murder mystery in a book. But I guess the author chooses what to tell us and the murderer is always some character in the story who doesn't seem a very likely suspect. I can usually figure out who the murderer is when I'm reading a mystery, but, of course, that's not what would happen in real life. The only people I know well are the people who live and work here."

"Life is stranger than fiction," a little voice warbled behind us, and Seatie's shadow, Mrs. T, eased herself down at the table with us, and I nodded and agreed that it was so true. Mrs. T wore a becoming pale blue cotton blouse over grey slacks today, which made me realize that I couldn't remember seeing any other women wearing slacks in the residence, and certainly not jeans, either. Maybe when I grew old enough to check out seniors' accommodations for myself, I had better remember to ask about dress codes.

Seatie showed Mrs. T the Rinehart book and reminded her of what a wonderful, thoughtful person I was and how thrilled she was to have a new author to read, and then started all over again on the subject of "wonderful Rachel."

As much as I enjoyed hearing this, after a minute or two, I began to wonder how to interrupt the flow of words from Seatie and make my request to be introduced to Marianne, assuming she was somewhere around. Before I could figure out how to solve this problem, Mrs. T looked over at me and interrupted Seatie with, "Jody might have been on her way to see the printer in your building to arrange some new menus. I heard Jody and Jake, the cook, talking about printing new menus that very Monday. Jody said she would go to the print shop and look at some designs." And then, with an abrupt jump shift, added, "I don't understand about that courier. Has anyone figured out why he was killed?"

I listened to this amazing statement about Jody's motive for going to the Ullman Building and wondered if Mrs. T or anyone else had mentioned it to the police. I stored the information away to tell Mitch the next chance that I had. Mrs. T was waiting for my answer to her question and I complied: "There is some possibility that the courier was killed only because he surprised a man who was stealing a company cap and clipboard from a Hasty X truck. It might have been the killer's attempt at using a simple disguise to get in and out of the Ullman Building, but, of course, no one really knows for sure, and it doesn't actually explain anything."

"How very peculiar," breathed Seatie. "Did anyone see a courier in your building who might have killed Jody?"

"A woman in the printing shop saw a Hasty X courier in the building at lunch time. Whoever it was didn't pick up or deliver anything to anyone who will admit to it." I decided not to mention that David Parker was also in the building at the key time, since they both probably knew that, nor did I tell them that our landlord, Karl Ullman, who may have been amorously involved with Jody, had also been hanging around for some reason. This whole thing was getting much too complicated.

Seatie, looking behind me, suddenly smiled at someone and said, "Oh, you must meet a new, young friend of mine." I turned, and there was Guy Levasseur, not in uniform, standing right behind me and in the company of an older man. They must have been coming up (or maybe it was considered "coming down") the hall, and recognized me as a tenant of the

Ullman Building, and perhaps even knew about the proposed article about The Manor. Seatie made the introductions. The second man, with white, thinning hair and a friendly grin in a heavily lined face, was probably in his late sixties or even his early seventies and turned out to be Jake Purcell, the cook. I had now met all the principals at The Manor, except for the elusive Marianne.

"I'm so pleased to meet you both," I said turning to focus on Guy, "I also want to meet your wife Marianne. The Manor is being featured in the December issue of *The Magazine for Island Business*, and I'm the one who will be writing the article. I've already interviewed Katherine Parker and will be talking to David tomorrow, and these two ladies have kindly agreed to be in one of the photos that we will probably use. I thought it might be a good idea to talk to Marianne as one of the managers so that I can offer some background information for our readers who will want to know what it's like to live here as well as hear the business case for owning a retirement residence. Marianne wouldn't have to worry that she would be quoted without a chance to review what is attributed to her. When I use quotes, I always ask for permission first, and allow the person I've interviewed to read what I've written before publication."

"Sounds okay to me," said Guy, his smile deepening. His shave was close, and he wore his dark hair neatly trimmed. In fact, his hair was so dark with such uniform color, I realized that he probably colored it himself, unlike his wife whose hair was graying naturally. Up close, he and Marianne looked much the same age and, if she were older, it couldn't be by more than a year or two.

"I'm sure Marianne would love to talk to you. She took a group of ladies out for lunch and a tour today—I'm picking them up in a couple of hours—but I'll let her know that you want to talk to her. Give her a call or drop by."

"I'll do that," I said. Nuts. I wasn't going to have a chance to talk to her before my interview with David.

Guy then added, "Has anyone given you a tour of The Manor yet?"

"Yes, Katherine took me around, and I've also seen Seatie's lovely apartment."

Guy looked disappointed and then brightened. "Have you seen Jake's stamping grounds? The kitchen?"

"No, I haven't."

"Well, come along with us now. You must see the kitchen, right, Jake?"

Jake nodded, looking pleased.

I bid a hasty goodbye to Seatie and to Mrs. T. "I'll have to get back to work right after my tour of the kitchen, but I'll be over to visit with you again soon," I said, moving off with the men.

The kitchen was big and impressive, and Guy conducted the tour, doing all the talking while Jake followed us around, helpfully opening cupboards and drawers to display their contents in Guy's wake. These were a couple of nice men who obviously enjoyed working in the residence and were well aware of the importance of their respective roles. Or so they seemed. I decided not to jump to any conclusions. When an opportune moment presented itself—meaning that Guy finally paused for breath—I turned to Jake and said, "I understand that you occasionally have new menus printed at the shop in the Ullman Building. Someone told me that Jody was probably on her way to the printer to check out designs for a new menu the day she was killed."

Jake hesitated, but answered easily enough, "I really don't think that's likely. Jody told me there was some money available to order new menu covers for the Christmas season, but that's still a long way off. She wouldn't have been worrying about Christmas yet."

"I must have misunderstood," I said. "I was told that you and Jody decided she should go to the print shop last Monday."

"No, we were talking about the Christmas menu covers. Nothing was really decided. The old folks here don't miss much, but they often misinterpret. None of us has any idea about what took Jody over to the building that day." He looked off into the distance and shook his head.

I thought back to what Mrs. T actually said and wondered if Jake and Guy had overheard our conversation. Even if they didn't, Jake obviously assumed that one of the residents had given me this information, and didn't care. Both men must be used to the gossip that would go on in a community like this one. Unfortunately, at that moment, I happened to glance up and see a great long line of knives of every shape and size held by their steel edges against a magnetized strip of metal screwed to the wall behind three cutting boards and a metal counter. No matter what you needed to slice, dice, shave, chop, mince, cube, or pound, this kitchen would have the perfect knife for the job. A number of them looked identical to me.

I was nervously trying to think of what to ask, but Guy saw me looking at the knives and jumped right in. "After the police showed up to ask David to go with them to the police station, a couple of cops came in here to examine these knives up here and they asked Jake if any were missing. Can you believe that? As if David would steal a knife from the kitchen and go and murder a nice girl like Jody. David really liked Jody; everybody knew that," Guy said, his voice rising in volume with each sentence.

I looked at Jake, and he shrugged. "I couldn't help the police with the knife question," he said. "I inherited a set from the cook who used to work here. He passed away, and no one from his family wanted his knives and so they are still here." He nodded to the knife display. "There are also quite a few that were bought as part of the original kitchen equipment and, of course, I brought my own when I came. Cooks like their own knives— instruments of the trade, so to speak—and none of mine are missing; however, I can't speak for the rest of them. I sometimes grab any knife and use it, but for the most part, I stick to my own," and he pointed to a group at one end, near the stove. "I've never bothered to do an inventory. I know my own knives and I'll take them with me whenever I leave here. Of course, since there was no knife inventory, I've been asked to make one now. As if I have time for that nonsense." He shook his head and made a face.

"So, you have to lock the barn door even though the horse may have already escaped?" I asked.

Jake's eyes glinted in appreciation, but he said only, "That's about it."

Guy broke in. "Do you know how the investigation is going? We haven't learned much except that the police are questioning the landlord of your building now. The newspapers said only that the investigation is continuing. Marianne and I went to Jody's funeral in Vancouver, and her mother asked if the police had the caught the wicked devil who killed her daughter, and, of course, we couldn't tell her anything new."

"I don't have much information either," I admitted. "I guess we won't know anything for sure until the police actually have a case against someone."

Guy's face darkened. "They'd better get a move on. It's a terrible thing when someone young and sweet like Jody isn't safe in a good neighborhood like this one. We thought the world of Jody, right, Jake?"

"You bet," came the reply. Jake had picked up a dishtowel and began idly wiping the pots upended on the counter near the institution-sized dishwasher. He stacked them near one of the ceiling-high cupboards but kept glancing at Guy who was fidgeting restlessly as he talked, running his fingers through his hair, patting his pockets, picking up and replacing odds and ends sitting on the counter.

"Jody was so young and pretty," Guy repeated heatedly. "She didn't deserve to die, and certainly didn't deserve to die the way she did, right, Jake?"

Again Jake agreed, but looked a bit concerned as he glanced at Guy. He then flicked a quick look at me and immediately turned his head. Obviously, it didn't take much to make Guy lose his cool, and Jake seemed a little worried about my witnessing it. On the other hand, Guy made no attempt to conceal his attraction to Jody. Wouldn't he be more careful about what he said if there had been more to it than the normal interest a male of any age has in a pretty woman?

I looked at my watch and declared my need to get back to work, which was certainly true. I thanked the two men, shook hands, and escaped. Had I learned anything important? Hard to say. Jake might have known that Jody had gone to the Ullman Building to see about a printing job and was lying. But why? Maybe there was a knife missing from the kitchen and Jake knew and was lying about that, too. Or perhaps he wasn't lying about anything. Mrs. T might have heard only half the conversation between Jake and Jody and didn't realize that they were talking about the distant Christmas menu, not something more immediate. It is entirely possible that a knife was missing from the kitchen and Jake didn't notice—there must be twenty, or so, knives hanging there—or perhaps none of the knives was missing. Guy might talk enthusiastically about his admiration for Jody because he believes a good defense is a good offense. If he actually pursued Jody, successfully or otherwise, he may have decided to admit to admiring her since it was no secret. Or maybe what he said was the simple truth; he liked her, thought she was pretty, and that was that.

Yes, I had gained some information but nothing very useful; I obviously needed to hone my skills as a detective. It was good to be going back to the office where I could demonstrate my ability to identify a dangling modifier and lay out ad copy like the pro that I was.

-12-

When the day finally ended, I drove to the nearby Town and Country Mall to find a present for Donna's youngest who was celebrating his birthday next week. The trip would justify the main event, which was checking out a sale on sweaters I had seen advertised. I refused to let myself think about Kevin's van being found in the parking lot such a short time ago and what it signified.

The mall was busy, and the shops crowded for this time of day. I was surprised until I finally noticed the series of discount signs proclaiming customer appreciation week, which had started the previous Friday. Apparently it was the anniversary of the opening of the mall five years earlier, and stores responded with various sales and discounted prices. I must have missed that particular flyer. It could only mean that my life was much too busy, and the police had better hurry up and bring our murderer to justice so that I could get back to the important things in life, like updating my wardrobe.

I found my way to the bookstore, and it wasn't too difficult to select an appropriate book and birthday card for Sean's birthday but, when I finally tracked down the sweaters, I sighed when I saw a gaggle of anorexic teenage girls trying them on. Not my style, obviously. I checked out a few more stores to see if I could help the mall celebrate their big event but sale bins and racks had already been well picked over and the most popular sizes and brands were gone. I finally decided that Sean's birthday card and book would be my only contribution to the mall's festivities, and when I headed home to my apartment, it was well past the dinner hour.

Along with the new book and a comical birthday card for Sean, I carried home the article I had written about Stuart's company. I still needed to polish it, but decided to let him read what I had written so far and make sure I was accurately describing the job of an actuary in layman's terms. I didn't even have to arrange the meeting. I had just reached the tea drinking stage after consuming a very large Caesar salad topped with shrimp when I heard a knock at my door. I looked through the security peephole and there he was. Just the man I wanted to see. And I made that announcement as soon as I opened the door.

Stuart smiled and shifted his body awkwardly. "I know you leave work pretty late sometimes," he explained, "and I wanted to make sure you were home now that it's dark. I mean …," he hesitated a minute. "I wanted to see how you were coming along with the article. You did say that you might have some more questions to ask…"

I was touched. The man was worrying about my safety. Why couldn't Donna find someone like this? I must find a good excuse for bringing them together.

"I don't actually have any questions at this point," I said, gesturing for him to enter and take a seat at the table. "However, I have a rough draft and I want to make sure I've described your work accurately. Let me get another cup and you can help me finish off this pot of tea. Or would you like some wine? Do you prefer white or red?" I added quickly, remembering that I had given him no choice last time.

"Oh, no, tea is fine," he said settling himself at the table. I fetched another cup, poured some milk into a small pitcher and grabbed the sugar bowl and carried them to the table. I poured Stuart some tea and refilled my own cup before searching for his article in my backpack.

"Here it is," I said at last, but when he reached for it, I paused. "It's just a rough draft. I have more work to do on it."

"I know all about rough drafts," he said, his arm still outstretched, his hand open. "That's all I ever produce. I always pass along my reports for someone else to clean up. I'm not an editor; it will look fine to me."

I nodded and handed the article to him. At least I hadn't doodled any cartoons on it or scribbled a shopping list in any of the margins. I settled back and sipped my tea while Stuart bent over the pages. I was pleased to see there was no pen in his hand.

When he finally looked up, he gave me a broad grin. "I like it. You make actuaries sound almost human."

"You seem almost human," I laughed.

"The jokes are a good touch. I would change this a bit," he pointed to one of the paragraphs. "That's maybe a little strong. We aren't really infallible, and that kind of suggests we might be."

I read the offending paragraph and nodded. "Okay, I'll tone it down a bit. Is my description of the reliance of accountants and actuaries on each other's work stated correctly? Do you think an accountant would accept that as properly described? I have to please them, too, if Donna is to have a hope of selling any ads around this."

"Sure," he said. "You won't get any argument from an accountant about it."

I sighed, relieved. "Good. And thanks for your help." I folded the article up and stuffed it back into my pack. "We still haven't been able to make the decision about using it in December or saving it now for the February issue. However, it's a great relief to have a lead article 'in the hamper,' so to speak. We aren't usually so well organized."

"That's fine, just fine. Use it whenever you like," Stuart said, accepting another cup of tea. He hadn't touched the cream or sugar, and I made a mental note to remember that for next time. "How are things going for you? Are the people in your building still feeling pretty threatened about what happened? Are the police keeping an eye on things?"

I thought that one over. "We haven't seen the police around for a few days, but I assume they are still checking things out. I guess you heard they took the landlord of our building in for questioning?" I turned the statement into a question and Stuart gave an affirmative nod. "They haven't laid any charges that I know about, and I am sure his lawyer will have arranged for him to be released by now. Anyway, I'm finding it hard to believe that Karl Ullman could be a murderer. I wouldn't be surprised if he walked away from this, and we'll be no farther ahead."

"He was such a quiet, nice guy, who kept to himself," Stuart quoted dryly—an irritating comment that seems to be a standard remark made by the neighbors of unmasked serial killers.

"No, that's just it," I answered. "He isn't quiet or nice, and Donna and I would like him a lot better if he *would* keep to himself. He's in our faces, insensitive, irritating, drooling over every female he comes in contact with…" I stopped short.

Stuart raised his eyebrows.

"Okay," I went on. "That doesn't sound good, but I really do think he's harmless. He's so 'out there,' if you understand what I mean, and he's all talk. What you see is probably what you get."

"I guess it's all right to trust your instincts about people most of the time," he said slowly, "but this is a situation where you have to be especially careful. Even if the police release him, it might be wise to keep your distance for a while."

"We'll certainly be doing that," I said, sipping my tea. "We don't even need an excuse."

"So, how is your family?" I continued, deciding it was time to change the subject. "You have two little granddaughters, don't you?"

"Yes, and they're fine, thank you, and growing very fast. I'm in the process of recording some bedtime stories for them. My daughter is a working mom, and like most working mothers is often exhausted in the evening. She really appreciates my going over there to help out at bedtime when her husband is out of town and I usually read the girls a story whenever I do. However, it occurred to me that I could find a couple of storybooks and record them, and then when I can't go over and read to them and my daughter wants a night off, she can put my CD in the player and the girls will have a storybook to look at while listening to me. I'm even inserting a few questions about the story just as I would if I were actually with the girls."

"What a great plan," I exclaimed, impressed. "Maybe I could do the same thing for my nephew, Josh."

"You could and it's really very easy. I've since heard that there are kits with books and CDs and instructions on how to record them, but there is nothing complicated about the job if you know how to use a computer. I didn't realize how much I would actually enjoy this project and I plan to have it finished and give a CD and some storybooks to my granddaughters this Christmas."

"Good for you."

We launched into a happy discussion about the exceptionally brilliant and beautiful young people in our families and Stuart brought out his wallet to show me the latest pictures, and I produced some of Josh. He finally looked at his watch and announced the time.

"I had better get home; I want to catch the news before I go to bed."

"I plan to turn on the news, too," I said, reluctant to have the pleasant evening end and knowing it would be some time before I could get to sleep. "Why don't you join me? I'll pour us some wine and you can turn on the TV. Would you like Chianti or a Chardonnay?"

"The Chardonnay, please," he said, after a brief hesitation. He rose to his feet and headed to where I was pointing at the remote.

We sat and sipped our wine as the sports, weather, and national news were presented, and then the local news began. We exchanged alarmed glances when the announcer told us in somber tones that another body had been found in Victoria under suspicious circumstances, and the police had not yet released any details. There was no reference to our two unsolved murders, but it was a cold comfort.

"Well," I said after a moment, losing all interest in following the subsequent boring updates on strike actions and government policy, "it might not be related at all."

Stuart was right with me and answered, "No, maybe not." He automatically muted the TV and stared at me for a moment. "Maybe you should stick pretty close to home until you know for sure."

"I'm being extremely cautious," I replied, "and suffering for it, too. I'm going to work earlier in the morning than I like because I've started leaving work when everyone else does. And I'm careful about where I park my car and where I walk, and, of course, this building is secure." I frowned. "As well, I can't think of one single reason anyone would want to get rid of me, including the fact that I have no idea who or what is behind the murders. I have no information that I haven't already babbled to the police, including everything I saw, heard, or even guessed at."

Stuart nodded and got to his feet. "Okay, but you had better continue to be very, very careful. Call me if you need me. I'm usually around."

We then said all the appropriate things about our evening together, went through our thank-you-very-muches, and I closed and locked the door behind him. I sighed and wandered back to the muted TV. Flicking through the channels, I found an old science fiction movie in progress that I had seen long ago, and settled into it. Why not? It's not like I could go to sleep yet.

I finally remembered my yoga breathing exercises when the credits started rolling, and did those, too, before I went to bed.

-13-

Carefully dressed for my interview with David the next morning in a pristine, white-trimmed navy pants suit, I drove directly to Evergreen Manor and selected one of several empty spots marked for guests in the parking lot. I suppose nine o'clock is too early for most visitors. I had forgone my usual cappuccino, assuming that I would be offered a cup of coffee from the seemingly endless supply produced for the seniors but, as I stepped out of the car feeling distinctly unnerved, I was sorry that I had been so shortsighted. I would have been much better off with some caffeine under my belt before tackling David. Clutching my notebook and with a small leather backpack slung over one shoulder, I scurried to the entrance of the building, wishing I had a lucky charm to ward off any evil spirits that might be lurking in the dark, brooding clouds that were crouching over The Manor. But when the first spatters of rain hit the ground as I reached the front step, I realized that the umbrella in the trunk of my car would have been more useful and was sorry that I didn't have sense enough to bring it with me.

I opened the massive, wooden front door trying to display more confidence than I felt, turned to my right, and stopped at the open office door. David was nowhere in sight, and Katherine was sitting at the front desk doing nothing at all. What was this? I gave a tentative knock, and she looked up, white to the lips. I stepped into the office and she motioned to the chair beside the desk. I didn't bother to speak as I sat down and waited for her to explain.

"They've taken David to the police station again," she said without any preliminaries. My jaw dropped. "Some woman who works in the Ullman Building was murdered last night, and David has no alibi."

Woman? Donna? My stomach lurched, and the darkness closed in around me—a dizzying array of dark purple spots whirling and enlarging— and I grabbed the arms of the chair, trying to remain upright as a ringing in my ears began and increased in volume, blotting out all other sounds. Suddenly, a vile odor assaulted my senses, and I became aware of a strong arm supporting me as I choked and spluttered, trying to catch my breath. The spots receded and the ringing diminished. When I could see and hear again, Katherine was leaning over me with an open bottle of smelling salts in her hand, and it was her firm arm around my shoulders that had kept me from sliding out of the chair.

"Who was murdered?" I managed as soon as I could speak.

"A woman who worked for that Paterson Printing Company in your building—Audrey Renwick or Rentick, or something like that," Katherine answered, removing her arm and straightening up now that I had obviously pulled myself together. She recapped the smelling salts and moved slowly back behind the desk, looking every inch her age. She sat down heavily. "They have decided to ask David more questions. He was home alone last night. He can't prove he didn't go out."

Audrey? Someone had killed Audrey? "That's not enough to hold him for long," I said finally, still holding on tightly to the arms of the chair, but having come to my senses with the realization that I would have been called if anything had happened to Donna. "Half the town wouldn't have had an alibi for last night."

"The police suspect him, not half the town," came the bitter reply. "His lawyer will get him released soon, but this thing is ruining his life. Karl Ullman was free yesterday, but, unfortunately for David, Karl has an alibi. This Audrey person was killed the same way Jody was killed, and it happened right outside her home, which is, to his great misfortune, not far from where David lives. It's within walking distance. I'm sure he's never even met her."

Of course, I was aware that whether David remembered Audrey or not, he had met her, and she certainly remembered him. What woman wouldn't? Also, Audrey told me she had seen David in the building that day and had had sense enough to tell the police as well. Why kill her now if that was the dangerous knowledge she had? What else did she know? Was she killed because she could identify the courier on the scene? But the courier couldn't have been David. What were the police doing? What had they learned that hadn't been made public? Did they suspect that David was deranged or something?

I wondered if "killed the same way" meant that a knife had been used, and if it was the same weapon that felled both Jody and Kevin. I pushed away a picture that leaped to mind of Audrey in her last moments of life. I looked instead at the stricken woman before me and was struck by a sudden wave of sympathy. How does any mother deal with her child being suspected of murder, or, even worse, forced to consider the possibility that the accusation is true? Was Katherine really convinced of her son's innocence?

I couldn't sit there all day debating with myself. I got to my feet, still feeling slightly wobbly. "Thank you for administering the smelling salts." I hesitated and then went on. "It's difficult to successfully prosecute even the guilty in our society. As uncomfortable and worrisome as this situation is, try to have faith that the universe will unfold as it should. I'll be in touch," I added, as I moved to the door, not able to think of anything less inane to say, and realizing nothing I said would matter to this self-absorbed woman anyway. Katherine didn't bother to reply, but looked up briefly to nod goodbye, and I got myself out of there, not sure I was fit to drive my car even as far as the adjacent parking lot.

I turned toward the front door but was halted by the sound of my name. "Rachel, Rachel!" I turned, and there was Mrs. T waving frantically from one of the tables. Did I want this right now? At least half of the residents were still in the dining room lingering over their breakfast coffee or tea, and I paused. The thought of a cup of coffee and the chance to sit quietly for a few more moments proved to be too much of a temptation. I made my way over to her table where she was seated alone and took a chair at a place where the breakfast dishes had already been removed. Mrs. T looked at me sharply and then raised her hand to signal one of the servers clearing the table next to us and motioned to her coffee cup and to me. It worked. A nice-looking young man—probably a university student working to pay his tuition—brought me a cup of coffee and pushed the sugar and cream pitcher toward me as I thanked him.

Mrs. T watched me take my first sip and nodded with satisfaction. I wondered if she would speculate on David having been taken in for questioning again. She must know about it; she noticed everything from her vantage point in the main room of the residence, and I wondered how many hours she actually logged in here. I waited for her to introduce the subject of David, or to inquire about my meeting with Katherine. She had obviously noticed that I was upset; however, having procured a cup of coffee to help me through my crisis of nerves, she promptly lost interest in whatever might have caused it. She began complaining, instead, about one of the ladies still eating her breakfast two tables away. "She is always one of the last people to arrive for breakfast," she said in an ordinary tone of voice, which I hoped didn't carry as far as the lady in question. "Can you imagine? Anyone who eats that slowly ought to get to the table as early as possible. All these nice young students have to get to classes today and she holds everybody up without so much as a twinge of conscience."

I glanced over at the young man clearing the next table who had brought my coffee and he grinned at me.

"She's just like my sister Martha," Mrs. T continued. "At home, my sister would talk all through the meal and then my mother would make everyone wait until she had finished eating before we could leave the table. It was downright inconsiderate. I mentioned it to my mother a number of times, but she just ignored me. Martha was at school with Katherine in Vancouver, you know."

No, I didn't know. Sister Martha must be a few years younger than Mrs. T. As though she had read my mind, Mrs. T gave me a conspiratorial smile, "I'm not as old as I look, and our mother was in her forties when Martha was born some years after me. Of course, Martha was pampered and spoiled and I guess I had a hand in that. She was much more talkative that I ever was and really shouldn't have been allowed to go on and on at mealtimes. She was younger, but she went before me just the same."

I realized she was telling me that her sister had died, and I slipped in an automatic, "I'm sorry to hear that," while Mrs. T's disjointed conversation continued to spill over me. I sat numbly sipping my coffee and felt myself gradually starting to relax. I was pleased when, without asking, the student server refilled my cup. "Thank you," I said again. "This is exactly what I needed." Audrey? Someone had killed Audrey?

"The uniform is what caused all the trouble, I'm sure," Mrs. T babbled on. "Uniforms are so attractive to women. I always say that you shouldn't trust a man just because he wears a uniform. That was Katherine's trouble, of course. Everyone knew she was making a mistake, but she wouldn't listen. Dazzled by a uniform, she was when a girl, and she fell head over heels in love. She fell in love with a uniform as far as I'm concerned."

I came back to earth with a jolt. What? What was she talking about? I focused on where she was gesturing to Guy and Jake chatting together outside the swinging kitchen doors. Neither was in uniform, of course. Why would Katherine's husband wear a uniform? He was a businessman, wasn't he?

"Are you still talking about Katherine? Who wore a uniform?"

But Mrs. T ignored the interruption. "How many times can you make the same mistake? She still loves a uniform, and people think I'm going soft in the head," Mrs. T giggled.

"Was Jake in the military or police force?" I asked, desperately trying to pull myself together and think of vocations requiring a uniform. "Are you talking about Guy and his chauffeur's uniform?" I ran through what I could remember of Mrs. T's monologue, trying to reconstruct it. Maybe I had just missed something important here.

But Mrs. T returned to her earlier topic and frowned at the little old lady still chewing on her toast. "Eats at a snail's pace, she does. Has no concern at all for these poor young men anxious to clear the tables and get to class. A snail, just like Martha." She took another sip of her own coffee, completely oblivious to the fact that she was guilty of the same lack of concern. "They're all university students, you know."

Suddenly, Mrs. T looked at her watch and exclaimed at the time. "I have to get ready to go. The van will be leaving soon. Seatie and I are going shopping, and she's already gone to her room to get changed. Mind you, I'm all ready to go. Except, maybe I need a jacket. Do you think I need a jacket?"

"It might be a good idea to take one, and an umbrella, too. It's started to rain," I said. "What uniform were you talking about?"

Mrs. T gave me a blank stare and didn't answer as she got up from the table. "It's been so nice talking to you, my Dear. I'm sure David will be fine." She turned and bustled off, leaving me with my mouth open.

Our helpful student server turned to the lady who was eating so slowly, addressed her by name in a friendly manner, and offered her more coffee. If his attitude was any indication, the students seemed to like the old people. They probably didn't have morning classes if they were serving breakfast and cleaning up afterwards.

I had no further excuse to sit there vegetating, and I managed to get myself out of the building and into my car, wheeling it around the manicured lawn and trees and into the Ullman parking lot without mishap. I could see a black-and-white as well as the now-familiar unmarked police car parked by the entrance to the building, and I braced myself for what was to come.

When I opened the office door, I found only three more people than usual, all of them clutching paper cups from our dispenser, very probably containing Cyndi's herbal tea. My glance slid past Mitch Williams, Bobby Kerr, and a uniformed police officer, and I spotted Donna by our office door with her hair standing on end where she had obviously been running her fingers through it. She gave me a brief, nervous, half-smile. Cyndi, standing by her desk, kept her big blue eyes firmly fixed on the face of the officer standing next to her with his notebook in hand.

Mitch turned from where he was facing Donna and my tears welled as soon as I caught his eye. He was with me in an instant. "I'm so sorry. Audrey Renwick was a good friend of yours?"

I shook my head and whispered, "I knew her only slightly, but when I heard it was a woman from our building, I was afraid it might be Donna. I learned almost right away that it wasn't but I'm still in shock, I think. Was it the same killer who … who …?"

"Ms. Renwick was killed in the same way, and we have good reason to believe it was probably with the same weapon. I hope you can remember anything more she might have said that could help us. She must have known something or seen something that she didn't realize was important. Donna and Cyndi say that they haven't spoken to her for a couple of weeks, and you are the only one who has. Her boss, Mr. Paterson, says they were always too busy in the shop to talk about anything but work. They were running behind on some orders, plus he was out of town for three days last week. He doesn't remember Audrey saying anything much about either murder. Perhaps when she spoke to family or friends, she casually passed along some information that she hadn't bothered to tell us. We're grasping at straws here."

I drew a deep breath and shook my head. "None of us in the office ever socialized with her, and she wasn't a very talkative person. I'm sure I've already told you everything I know. I didn't speak to Audrey again after I saw her in the parking lot last Wednesday and pushed her to tell me what the courier looked like. She didn't, of course."

"Do you suppose she actually recognized the man? Maybe she didn't want to make trouble for someone."

"That isn't the impression I had, but I don't know."

"Call me anytime day or night if you remember anything, anything at all."

The other two police officers were waiting for him now, and Mitch looked around the room, and repeated his message. "Silence can be dangerous. That's likely why this last murder has occurred. If you think of anything, call me or Constable Kerr. If you can't get to one of us right away, give your information to anyone who takes your call. And watch yourselves. We don't know what's going on yet, so, please, take every precaution for your own safety."

Everyone acknowledged his remarks with various head bobs and murmurs of agreement, and, satisfied, he strode from the office with his men following behind. I suddenly remembered something important that I hadn't asked, and I raced after them calling, "Back in a sec," over my shoulder.

The men were just at the top of the stairs, and I called to Mitch who waited for me. "Did you find anyone in the building who called a courier last Monday?" I asked.

"The financial advisor and the real estate agents received letters delivered by couriers that afternoon, but no one received anything from Hasty X morning or afternoon, and no one called a courier from the building."

I stood frowning and repeated my earlier statement: "Audrey said the courier was from Hasty Xpress when she first talked about it. Something must have suggested that to her no matter what she claimed later when asked."

Mitch sighed. "Yes, and she told us it was a courier she didn't recognize. She didn't specify Hasty X at that time. We asked her which company but she said she didn't know. Later, she wasn't even sure it was a courier."

"Audrey," I began, and then my voice broke and I had to start again. "Audrey was never sure of anything, and I'd be inclined to go with her first instincts. By the way, one of the residents at The Manor seems quite sure that Jody had planned to come over here on Monday to arrange the printing of some menus."

"Jody was coming to see Karl," Mitch frowned. "He told us that. She never arrived, and she was heading up stairs."

"Oh, yes, of course," I said, and stood there wondering if there could be any other explanation and hoping that he would mention why the police had centered their attention on David again, but Mitch merely thanked me and went on his way.

Back in the office, Donna was standing uncertainly over Cyndi who had collapsed in tears at her desk. "She wants to go home," Donna told me. "It's probably a good idea. We can manage without her today, can't we?"

"Yes, of course," I said. "You run along Cyndi. We'll be fine."

Cyndi sniffled her thanks and began her preparations to leave, and Donna and I moved quickly to the back office. But before we could even begin to compare notes on the recent developments, the phone rang. Donna, heaved a sigh, took the call and responded, "She's right here." She waved the phone at me, jabbed at the buttons to transfer the call, and I picked it up at my desk.

I heard a familiar voice, and an even more familiar line: "And he dried the joint on his long, blond hair."

"Ryan," I said and smiled, momentarily diverted. "So, what comes next?"

He replied, "I guess I know when I am beat;

It's time to call for a retreat."

What? Ryan said nothing more, and I paused, trying to puzzle out the lines, and wondered why he had called. Finally, I said, "I'm going to have to think about that for a while. Is there anything I can do for you?"

"No, but there's something I can do for you."

"What's that?"

"I'm with someone you might want to talk to."

"Where are you?"

Ryan named an address near the iron works, and added, "I'll be waiting on the street. You should maybe hurry to get here."

"I'm on my way. Give me fifteen minutes, or so."

"Hookay," came the answer.

As I hung up the phone, I pushed back from the desk and reached for my backpack. "I'm going out for about half an hour," I said to Donna, who was still waiting to talk over the latest frightening development in our neighborhood. "I'm going to meet a young man who works for a friend of mine. He knows something about the drug scene, and I want to check it out."

Donna, looking anxious, started to rise from her chair. "I'll come with you."

"No, no, don't worry. The young man's name is Ryan, and he's a friend. He'll look after me," I said confidently. "It will be better if I go alone."

Donna looked as though she were about to insist, but just then, the door to the outer office opened, and we both recognized the booming voice of one of our current advertisers. I stepped back so that Donna would precede me to the outer office, and, as she greeted the man standing there, I flashed him a smile, gave a wave of my hand, and darted out the door. Who knew how long Ryan could hang on to whoever it was? The rain had stopped, and I hurried over to my car, wheeled out of the lot, and drove as fast as I dared towards an industrial area of town. The street on which I expected to meet Ryan seemed deserted, although a few cars were around, presumably belonging to the people who worked near here. I could hear the thump and whine of machinery, and I wondered what was manufactured in these dismal surroundings. How could I know so little about the city in which I had lived for the last thirty years?

When I located him, Ryan was leaning up against a grubby brick building with his eyes closed. His face was tilted up as though to catch the single shaft of sunlight that had cut through the clouds and between the tall buildings. With his pale face framed by blond hair, he looked like some exotic flower turned to catch the warmth of the sun's rays. I parked my car as close to where he was standing as I could and carefully locked the doors behind me. As I approached him, Ryan opened his eyes and glanced in my direction. He pushed himself off the wall and turned toward a doorway on his right as a teenager stepped out into the street in response to a jerk of Ryan's head.

The boy, a skinny seventeen- or eighteen-year-old, shifted from one foot to the other, pulled his hands out of the pockets of his ratty jeans, patted his clothes here and there, and looked left, right, up, down—anywhere but at my face. In spite of the chilly day, he was perspiring freely, and he suddenly rubbed his face with grimy fingers leaving dark streaks along his nose and across his forehead. It didn't take any experience to see that this guy was high. He shoved his hands back in his pockets and stared to the left of my face.

"Tell her what you told me, Johnny," said Ryan, without bothering to supply introductions.

"Uh, yeah, well, I sometimes buy stuff from an old dude who told me that the folks at The Manor wouldn't miss it.

"What does he look like?" I asked.

"Just an old dude."

"How old?"

"I donno. Old."

"Is he about forty? Sixty? Eighty?"

"Yeah."

"Yeah, what? Forty? Eighty? Narrow it down for me."

"I never got a good look at him. He wears a hat. Just an old dude."

Which means the man could have been any age over thirty, I realized. I tried again. "How often do you buy from him? Every week?"

"Yeah, maybe. I donno." The boy shrugged. "I buy whenever he calls me. We meet."

"Where do you meet?"

"Uh, lots of places. We met here once, I think." The boy looked around him, vaguely surprised, as if he had just noticed where he was. "Yeah, we met here once. Yeah, here," he said again, as though to reassure himself.

"When was the last time you saw him?"

"I donno. A while ago."

"A few days ago or a few weeks ago?"

This question really stumped him, and he said nothing at all, and then finally shrugged. "I don' remember. A while ago."

"Is he as tall as Ryan?" I asked, deciding to try another tact. Ryan was standing quietly beside us, his face expressionless, and Johnny carefully checked out his height (about six foot) as though giving this question some careful thought. Or maybe he was falling asleep.

"How big is he? Is he as tall as Ryan?" I repeated.

The boy shrugged again. Probably too spaced out to notice at the times they had met and too spaced out now to remember anything very useful. "Middling height," he said finally.

So, not as tall as Ryan, then, which is more likely to mean Guy or Karl than David. Except that Karl had an alibi for the time that Audrey was killed, assuming our old dude and our killer are one and the same.

"So, the big question is, how old is an old dude?" I said, thinking aloud, and Ryan began to laugh, and kept laughing. I focused on him and noted his eyes with their pinpointed pupils for the first time, and realized with shock that he was high, too.

I turned back to Johnny and gave it a last try. "Is there anything you remember about the man that could help me identify him?"

The boy shrugged and looked up and down the street as though hoping the man we were talking about would miraculously appear. "It's always dark when we meet. I never noticed much," he said finally.

"Thank you for your help," I said, realizing this was probably the best he could do. At least I now had the drug connection that I had suspected all along. The police could follow up on this. I would tell Mitch about it.

The boy nodded and glanced at Ryan, who reached into his pocket and handed him a small package. I couldn't see what was in it, but realized what it must be. Johnny shuffled off without another word or glance at either of us, and Ryan immediately walked over to the doorway where the boy had been standing. He bent down and picked up a duffel bag and then turned back to me. I suddenly understood. Ryan was leaving town. He had his possessions with him, and was dressed as he had been when I first saw him. He had waited just long enough to provide this last service for me—his comrade of the rhyming couplet game. Those final lines delivered over the phone made sense now: "I guess I know when I am beat; it's time to call for a retreat." He was talking about himself.

"Did that help?" he asked.

"Yes, it helped. I really appreciate it, and I'm sorry you're leaving," I answered sadly. Ryan was getting too old to go on playing this game. How many more chances would he have to grow up and pull his life together? He must be in his late twenties by now, maybe even his early thirties. Time was running out for him.

"Ned never did have much luck," he said, hoisting his bag over his shoulder.

"Maybe not, but he has a good heart, and he can always change his luck," I said, wishing I could think of something more inspirational to say.

But Ryan seemed to think it was an appropriate send-off, and he gave me a crooked little smile before he walked away. I watched him for a moment, wondering if I should offer him a lift, and then realized he had probably made whatever arrangements he needed. If he wanted something from me, he would have asked. Was Hogg going with him? Had they both been fired? I would get the story from Mark or Tommy sooner or later. I sighed and walked back to the car.

The look of relief on Donna's face when I got back to the office was unmistakable. "Don't you do that to me again," she almost snarled, and I didn't have to ask what she meant. "I'm ordering a pizza and sodas for an early lunch for both of us. We need some decent sustenance."

I nodded with a "make it half cheese," and plunked myself down at my desk while she made the phone call. I kindly didn't suggest we share a bowl of cabbage soup in addition to the pizza. I was suddenly very tired.

After she placed the order, we sat for a moment in silence and then held our own private eulogy, exchanging our pleasant as well as humorous memories of Audrey. We finally wound it down, and Donna gave her shoulders a shake. "It's time you told me where you went this morning and what you learned."

I gave her all the details.

"Will the police will be able to track this kid down with your information, and do you think he will be capable of describing the 'old dude' any better for them?" Donna asked, her face still mirroring her shock at the revelation.

"I don't suppose it matters if he can describe the man or not. If the police know what is happening, they'll be able to turn up something. They will probably talk to their informants, or put the kid under surveillance. Johnny is probably a contact who receives money from someone to buy the drugs and then passes the stuff on. Someone else must have set up the exchange; Johnny seems too young and too clueless to figure out much of anything."

"So, are you going to call your Mitch and tell him about it right away?"

"He's not my Mitch, and I don't see that there's any immediate rush. I'll call him later this afternoon," I said absently, as the outer office door opened and the smell of pizza wafted towards us. Donna pulled open the petty cash drawer and looked after the business transaction.

When we were nicely occupied in wolfing down pizza and Cokes, she zoomed in on my reluctance to make an immediate phone call to Mitch. "So, how long will it take this Ryan character to get himself off the Island and safely out of harm's way?" she asked.

I shot her a look over a pizza slice dripping with cheese and slowly chewed and swallowed before answering. She waited. "I figure he's probably catching a ferry, and can disappear into the bowels of Vancouver by late afternoon," I said reluctantly. "If he had anything more useful than a casual statement he heard from that kid, he would have told me. He wanted to help, but even the kid didn't really know anything of value. There's no sense in mixing Ryan up in this."

Donna shook her head in mock despair. "And you tell me I'm nuts when it comes to men."

"How can I not lose my heart to a man who writes the same kind of rotten verse I do?" I grinned. "Besides, he's got gorgeous golden locks that both you and I would kill to have. That in itself should earn him a break. It's a great pity he's probably ten or fifteen years younger than I am, unemployed, and a druggy—otherwise, he's my kind of guy."

We snickered companionably and then quickly sobered up. It didn't seem to be a day for laughing at anything.

"She may never have realized what was happening," I said, knowing that Donna would immediately understand that I was referring to Audrey, "any more than Jody or Kevin would have known. That kind of death is really fast."

Donna nodded without saying anything, and we got back to work. My work included a phone call to Mandy to update her on the latest developments. I hoped that she would be at the shop and I could reach her before the news about Audrey's murder was being blasted out over her car radio when she was on her way to visit a client, or some other inconvenient moment. I was relieved when her assistant answered brightly and told me that Mandy was free and would be right with me. As soon as I heard her voice, I gave her a quick, condensed version of the situation. "I tried to push Audrey into making a better effort to recall and define what she had seen when I had that last conversation with her, but obviously failed," I finished up. "She preferred to put the whole thing out of her mind in order to avoid being involved, but apparently she saw more than she wanted to let on to the police, or to me, for that matter."

"And what did you see? Or, more importantly, what would the killer think you know?" Mandy asked, her voice tight.

"Not a thing," was my prompt answer. "I've not only told the police everything I heard and observed, but I've also provided them with endless speculation about what might or might not have happened, whether they wanted to hear it or not."

Mandy sighed. "I suppose there is no chance that you could take a bit of time off? You could come up here for a visit."

"No, there's no chance. But thank you, and I assure you that if I thought for one minute Donna or Cyndi or I were in any danger, we would close down the magazine for a month, or hire bodyguards, or something. The police are keeping a close eye on this building, and we are all being careful to watch out for ourselves and for each other." I continued to answer questions and offer reassurance for a few more minutes, but Mandy had an afternoon appointment and couldn't talk very long. We hung up after I promised to call as soon as I had any new information, and I spent the rest of the afternoon immersed in my editing and trying not to let thoughts of Audrey intrude.

Shortly before five o'clock, I made my call to the police and was able to reach Mitch.

"When was this and where?" he barked as soon as I had made myself understood.

I gave him the street address and told him I had talked to the boy today, carefully omitting the hour. I fully described the teenager who had been identified only as "Johnny" to me. "And good luck at getting anything more out of him than I did," I said. "He certainly didn't seem to be playing with a full deck. Not today, anyway. All I really learned is that, yes, someone has been selling drugs from The Manor, and how often is anybody's guess. It's a man identified by Johnny-of-the-scrambled-brains as an 'old dude,' who could be any age over thirty, I suppose, and he is of 'middling height.' It's not great, but it's a lead, at least."

"And the man who led you to Johnny? Who is he?"

"Oh, he's another young guy that I know slightly. He arrived in Victoria after the first two murders took place, and he was leaving town today. Called me on his way and led me to Johnny. I had told him and his friends I was looking for a drug connection and he wanted to help."

Mitch asked a few more questions but eventually realized I had told him all I could and he thanked me. Since he now owed me one, I quickly asked him if the police had uncovered any other love interests that Jody might have had, and if she really had been seriously involved with Karl.

"Yes, Jody was having an affair with Karl, and we're investigating a few other men and eliminating them one by one. No joy yet."

"And David Parker?"

"I can't tell you anything about David," Mitch answered gruffly. And before I could ask any more questions, he ended the call by reminding me to leave the investigation to the police and to quit messing around in something that could get me killed. But he said it quite nicely. After all, I had given him a valuable lead. How ornery could he afford to be? I smugly hung up the phone.

"Well done," Donna said, waiting for me to finish so that we could leave the building together. "May the bears never catch up with Goldilocks."

"Bulls, not bears. The police are always bulls."

"And you've supplied a little red herring for the bulls?"

"I haven't misled anybody."

"Technically, lying by omission could be considered a red herring."

We continued this petty and ridiculous wrangling all the way out to our cars. There were three vehicles still on the lot, and Karl's wasn't one of them. He was probably at home trying to charm his wife out of not walking out the door and taking half their assets with her. Donna and I carefully looked around us and checked over our cars, including the back seats, and without any discussion about it, we waited until both our engines had started and we were moving. We headed into the street, exchanged waves, and drove off in opposite directions. It was still daylight; we were still safe; and I had a mountain of work to tackle in the morning.

I was glad I made it home and was alone before the tears started. Whatever her shortcomings, Audrey was kind, friendly, and productive, and her life should not have ended as it did. I spent a long time on my yoga breathing exercises before retiring for the night.

-14-

Thursday morning started badly and went rapidly downhill from there. I had slept poorly and didn't get out of bed when the alarm sent out its shrieking notice that it was time to get up and face the day. When I finally crawled out to do just that, I had to rush like crazy and was already a half-hour late for work before I had even climbed into my car. As well, the sun was shining right in my eyes on the drive and I was annoyed to discover that I had left my sunglasses at home. Cyndi had called Donna at the office to announce that she was taking another day off work and Donna was so furious with her that she was curt to the point of rudeness when I arrived. I turned on my computer and started my work, while on the other side of the room Donna battled with her bookkeeping and the constant phone interruptions. There was no friendly banter to lighten the morning.

At about eleven-thirty, I thought to check my calendar in case anything important was lined up for the day that I had forgotten about. I noted the date and the printed notation beneath it and read aloud, "Today is the anniversary of the death of American saxophonist Lee Allen."

"Oh, sure," said Donna, who wouldn't have known who Lee Allen was or cared if she did know, "and no one bothers to mention it to me until the day is half over."

I turned my head and opened my mouth for a friendly snicker, but the sound that came out was a strangled shriek. I had suddenly caught sight of a large, red spider moving rapidly down the wall behind Donna, and I leapt to my feet, pointing at it with a trembling finger and managed to bang my head on Cyndi's stupid hanging plant for the second time. Donna pulled off her shoe and held it aloft ready to administer a swift death, but the spider was too fast for her and disappeared behind the baseboard.

She looked back at me contritely as she bent down to replace her shoe. "Sorry about that. I tried."

I stood there rubbing my head where I had banged it, and she suddenly snarled, "That's it for that ridiculous hanging plant of Cyndi's. We're getting rid of it before you wind up with a concussion."

"We can't do it today. Cyndi is the only one who knows how to find a ladder in this stinking firetrap. And have you noticed anyone who looks like fire inspector—so thoughtfully summoned by Karl—hanging around the building this week?"

"Are you kidding? Karl probably arranged all these murders just to scare him off."

We both started to laugh, but within seconds, I was crying. Donna grabbed the box of tissues and touched me gently on the shoulder. I said between sobs, "When I first heard that a woman who worked in this building was murdered, I was afraid it might be you. I haven't recovered."

"Hey," said Donna, cheerfully handing me a tissue and giving me a hug, "do you think I would let myself be killed and leave you with no ads for the December issue?"

"That wasn't it," I said, calming down. "It made me remember that we have never taken out business owner's insurance on each other's lives, and we should hurry up and do that." We both managed to react to that in the usual way, although our laughs were a little shaky. I took a deep breath and added in a whisper, "When it turned out to be Audrey, I was so relieved. I can't get over feeling guilty about it."

"Yes, you can," Donna answered calmly. "You weren't relieved it was Audrey; you were merely relieved it wasn't me. You know that. Say it."

Tears welled up again, but I obediently repeated, "I wasn't relieved it was Audrey. I was relieved it wasn't you," and I managed to smile through my tears.

Happy that I showed signs of pulling myself together, Donna came up with her usual solution to a crisis. "We need to eat. Something really tasty and bad for us. I'm going to go out and get us some hamburgers and fries."

"Great, make mine a chicken burger and hold the fries," I said, and off she went. I looked doubtfully at the baseboard where the spider had disappeared, gave myself a shake, and returned to my computer.

Later, when we were both relaxing over our "tasty-and-bad-for-us" lunch, we decided that we should make some effort to decide who were the most likely candidates for Killer of the Month so we could be on our guard. Donna took a shot, but got nowhere. She favored Karl.

"Out of the running," I interrupted before she could launch into her justification, and added, "He couldn't have killed Audrey; he evidently has an alibi. I heard it from Katherine, and he wasn't taken for questioning again by the police. The authorities must be satisfied with his alibi and we could hardly have two killers racing around using the same weapon."

"Fine. Let's hear your theory."

But I didn't want to build a case against David and have Donna convince herself he must be innocent by defending him against anything I said. Anyway, I wasn't sure he was guilty, and so, in the time-honored fashion, I waffled. "Stuart says we should look for the common denominator," I said.

"Our actuary? What did he mean by that?"

"I think he meant that we should look at something the victims all have in common, or anyone they all could have known. Anyone who could have killed all three fits into the pattern and is someone we must be careful to avoid—day and night. Let's do that. We'll use our little grey cells in the true Hercule Poirot fashion, and I'll write everything down," I said and brushed the crumbs off my fingers. Turning to my computer, I opened a new document.

"Okay," Donna said, instantly in the game as I sat with my fingers poised over the keys. "What have we got here? One victim was male and two were female. The male was in his twenties; there was a female in her thirties and another in her forties. The male was married with two children, and the two females were single. We have a courier, an administrator in a seniors' residence, and a printer's receptionist-assistant. I noted from the newspaper articles that they all lived in different parts of town." She paused. "Have you got all that?"

"No, but I just noticed a flaw in all this. There was probably only one real target, and the others were just killed because they were dangerous to the killer. They knew something, or the killer thought they did, or they simply had something needed by the killer, which was maybe the case with Kevin, the courier. Kevin's characteristics are not important if he was killed only because he could identify the person stealing his cap and clipboard in order to get into the building. It's not common characteristics of the victims on which we should focus; there must be something else in common that they all shared."

"The building," said Donna thoughtfully. "The Ullman Building. That must be the connection. Audrey worked here; Jody came here sometimes; and Kevin made deliveries here. Everyone who died had some reason to be in here."

"That's true," I said, starting another list. "Were they all acquainted? No, Audrey and Jody knew each other, but we haven't found any connection between Jody and Kevin, and Audrey may not have recognized Kevin even though she must have seen him now and then."

"Maybe not," said Donna. "He wasn't delivering here for very long, was he? How long had he been coming to our building?"

"I have no idea. We'll have to ask Cyndi."

"You mean we won't have solved this whole thing after making our lists?"

"I'm the one typing my fingers to the bone. You concentrate on keeping it coming."

"Okay, let's try another angle. Who would or could come to our building and either knew all three or would run into all three?"

"No," I stopped typing and shook my head. "This is becoming too broad. Let's concentrate on the people who might be interested in killing Jody. We should go through those names. Audrey's and Kevin's murders are likely to have been incidental."

"True," Donna sighed. "What names should we add from The Manor?"

"Besides David, there is Guy the manager, and Jake the cook."

"We shouldn't be so quick to eliminate the women. Maybe a knife isn't the usual weapon for a woman, but it's not impossible, is it? So, add Katherine and that other woman—the one married to Guy."

"Marianne."

"Right, Marianne. How closely have the police been looking at the other people in this building? Maybe we are wrong about Mr. Paterson, the printer. Maybe he's a psychopath and kills for no reason. And the real estate agents and fat Garth downstairs would have known Audrey, and maybe knew Kevin and Jody, too. We haven't seriously considered them, have we?" Donna said with sudden excitement.

I paused again. "I'll add the names Katherine and Marianne. I don't know Marianne, but it's pretty ridiculous to include Katherine. You should have seen her the morning the police took David to the station again. She was a broken woman. Would she do anything to risk his safety? I don't believe it; I really don't believe it. If she killed anyone, she would have made sure it was at a time that David had an alibi. And if you could see the shoes Marianne wears, you wouldn't want her on the list either. Sensible oxfords. No one who wears sensible oxfords could take a knife to anyone."

"I don't understand why you're working on a magazine when your real calling is consultant to police forces. The things you know about the criminal mind take my breath away."

I ignored her and went on: "We haven't taken a serious look at Paterson or the real estate guy, whose name is Mark something, if you'll recall, or his partner, Marcia, but you may be sure the police have. They will also have all pertinent information about fat Garth, too, including his exact weight. I'll add their names, but the police will have done a background check on everyone by now. If they didn't have alibis, the police would have taken one or all of them in for further questioning, and we would have heard about it. The police know all about us, too, and you should be very grateful that I supplied you with an airtight alibi. All your guilty secrets are in a police file downtown, you may be sure."

"And boring reading it will be, God save us all here," Donna said with a regretful sigh.

"Mr. Paterson has closed up the printing shop for the remainder of this week, by the way. He's going to be lost without Audrey."

"Yes, poor man. Have you heard when her funeral will take place? We'll have to attend. And what about Kevin Lewis's funeral? Should we go to it as well? The newspaper said that it would be held this Saturday."

"Cyndi is the only one of us who really knew him and she said she was going. She can represent our office. But, yes, we'll go to Audrey's funeral, which will probably take place next week."

Donna sighed again.

"Do you realize what we've overlooked here? The important drug connection, that's what," I said triumphantly. "We have to work that in, and that means we need a list with only men from The Manor on it for that category. After all my efforts to prove there is a connection, we can't ignore that fact."

"Except we can't overlook the possibility that it's not someone who works there but who lives there—some very old but kinky resident. Have you met any of the old boys?"

"No, I haven't," I sighed. "Maybe we're wasting our time with this. Maybe the killer will turn out to be some derelict druggy who just wanders around killing people for the fun of it and has already moved on."

"Like your Ryan has moved on?" Donna suggested.

"No, not like my Ryan has moved on," I said, turning around to give her the full blast of my scowl. "Give it up. We wouldn't have learned about the drug connection without him, remember? The police found nothing when they looked into it. I asked questions of some young guys that I know, and Ryan just happened to be there at the time—he and his buddy arrived in town after the first two murders took place—and when he discovered a source of information, he told me about it. Can you think of any good reason for Ryan to lead me to that boy if he, himself, were involved in some way? Face it; he didn't just tell me what he heard; he arranged to have me meet the boy. Like it didn't occur to him that I could and would identify the boy to the police? He was well aware of that. That's why he got me down there. He's a software developer and tester; he's not stupid. And even if he had a motive and came to town the day before the murders took place, and then left and came back just to cover his tracks, how did he get into our building without being noticed? Do you think he could have pulled up his hair and tucked it under a cap? His hair is so long, the cap would have been balancing a foot above his head. He wouldn't have had to kill Audrey if she saw him, she would have died laughing on the spot."

Donna threw up her hands. "Okay, okay, I give up. So, what do you have there? Anything that helps?"

I looked back at my lists. "I'd say, for our safety, we must avoid any male connected with The Manor. I suppose we should be careful about the two women, even though I can't believe they are involved in any way, but on general principles. If someone wants to meet with you, make sure it's daylight, there are people around, and someone is with you. Also, we should make sure no one is alone here—day or night—unless the door is locked. As well, the police can make mistakes or, as is sometimes the case, they've figured out who the killer is, but don't have the evidence to hold him. As well, you're probably right about the people who work in this building. Let's not assume anyone has actually been cleared."

"Not even Karl with his alibi?"

I hesitated. "Not even Karl," I said reluctantly, remembering that David may be released again, and Donna might decide to take that as a sign that he was innocent if I declared Karl to be innocent. "Better not eliminate anyone at this stage. I'll add Karl's name to the list," and I sent out a mental apology to him.

"What are your conclusions about all this, Rachel?" Donna asked. "You think you know who did this, don't you?"

"No, I don't. But I've pieced together some of it and that is why I'm particularly concerned about the men. Forget the motive and just consider the chain of events. We should be able to assume that Jody was the main target. The killer probably knew about Karl and Jody's affair, and I believe he killed Kevin so that he could be in the building unnoticed using Kevin's cap and clipboard to pass himself off as a courier. All three people were killed the same way and with probably the same knife. That is why, according to this line of reasoning, we shouldn't have to worry about Katherine or Marianne because the killer must be a male. Add to that the fact that a knife, statistically, isn't likely to be used by a woman, and if a woman did use one, she would be more likely to stab her victim rather than cut his or her throat."

I went on when Donna made no comment. "This man might have known Kevin personally, and it is someone who can drive a van. He also knew that Jody came to our building now and then. Perhaps Jody came to visit Karl on certain days, and the killer was in a position to know that. He killed Kevin, and later, shoved the knife in the ground somewhere that he could retrieve it easily. He added Kevin's cap to whatever he was wearing. Perhaps it was a uniform, too, but it didn't have to be. He entered the building and waited for Jody to arrive, or he followed her and caught up with her at the stairs. Audrey noticed him in the building at some point, and she had to be eliminated because she might be able to identify him if she ran into him again. He had to make his move on her as soon as he could. How did he find out about her? Maybe he got a glimpse of her himself or heard that Audrey mentioned there was a courier in the building, and he was afraid that his thin disguise wasn't enough. I mentioned that Audrey had seen a courier when I was at The Manor, and I'm sure I was overheard by both Guy and Jake, and might have been overheard by others, too. Perhaps other people learned about it and anyone could have mentioned this to David. I'm not saying David is the most likely suspect; I'm just saying any man from The Manor could have been here, and we know that David was. In any case, the connection is the Ullman Building and The Manor. If Jody had some former lover who is behind this, the police haven't found him, and yet he is either living in, or close to, The Manor and was able to connect to Jody—could follow her and learn her movements. And, of course, if you throw in the motive, there's another possibility altogether."

"What's that?"

"The first one that we came up with a few days ago. A woman steals drugs from The Manor and a male colleague sells them. He had a reason to kill Jody, who may have been the thief in spite of what the police think."

"God save us all here, don't tell me this. We're back to Karl."

"Get off the Karl kick; it could be any male. I think the common denominator is the geographic location, and the motive could be love or money, meaning drugs or even blackmail. Maybe Jody did have lots of money hidden somewhere and the police just haven't found it yet."

Donna heaved a big sigh. "You're probably right. I guess we have to be especially careful until the police finish their job. What if they never solve this?"

"They have to," I answered grimly. "They probably have a lot of leads, and they now have a drug connection to follow up. Little by little, they will be able to eliminate people and whoever is left is the right one. This whole thing started only a week ago Monday. Give them some time."

"I suppose you can't leave early today? I can't look at these books any longer, and the phone hasn't rung for a couple of hours."

I sat and thought a moment and finally made my announcement. "I hate to tell you this, but I not only can't leave early, I should stay late or I should come back after dinner."

"No, you can't. I won't let you."

"Look, I can't do this work at home, and we have a business that we can't simply put on hold. The print deadline is approaching, and I've taken a lot of time off recently, including this last hour as we sat here and tried to figure out the identity of our neighborhood killer. I've known all along it would come to this and the time has arrived. I need to work late tonight and tomorrow night and through the weekend. I'll take every precaution for my safety, but I need to do this."

"No, no," said Donna, "I'll come back here tonight with you."

"My calendar noted that the anniversary of the death of Lee Allen is today, but there is another important event taking place on this date. Your son Pat is playing his first hockey game of the season tonight, remember? I was hoping to go and watch him, too, but he'll be really disappointed if you aren't there. You can't spend your evening babysitting me. I'll be safely locked in here."

Donna jutted her jaw out stubbornly. "But you would be leaving here after dark when no one else is in the building. You'll be all alone in the parking lot. How can you consider taking such a chance? Or maybe while you're here, you'll get hungry and will order in food. You'll watch for a delivery van and run downstairs when you see it. The knock will come at the door and you'll open it to a freaking killer instead of the delivery boy. I can see it all now."

"What happened to my delivery boy?"

"What do you think? Figure it out."

Her brow furrowed. "Okay, let's make a sensible plan to cover all contingencies. Let's leave together now. You have your dinner and do whatever. I have to have Patrick delivered to the arena by six-thirty. I'll swing by your apartment building about six-fifteen and the boys and I will wait for you in the parking lot. You come down at that time, and before we go to the arena, we'll drive you here and see you safely into the building.

I'll give you a minute to get up to the office, and you flick the lights when you are in here and have the door locked. We'll go on to the game, and Pat will be on the ice from seven to eight. By the time he gets changed and out of the dressing room and we get all his hockey gear in the car, it will be going on nine o'clock. So, we could be back here just after nine. I'll call you when I'm in the parking lot and you come down. Will that give you enough time?"

I shook my head. "I was thinking more along the lines of working until about midnight tonight—especially if I'm going to go home and have dinner. I should work late tomorrow night, too, but I could bring something from home so that I won't be tempted to order any fast food. On the weekend, I'll work from nine-thirty to, say, four-thirty on Saturday and Sunday, and that should put us in good shape for the deadline. I may have to work late one more night next week; it depends on what last minute things go wrong—you understand. I'll know the day before and we can plan something for that night."

We could hear the comfortable sounds of people and activity in the Ullman Building: a door banged; someone was laughing. Everything seemed so safe and familiar, but I knew it wouldn't feel that way when the building emptied. The exodus started about four-thirty, and the building was usually empty by five-thirty. "I really can't leave this early, but I can certainly get myself out of here before five o'clock when most people in the building are still here. Then, I could go home and have my dinner as you suggest. I'll drive my own car back here with you and the boys riding shotgun in your car. Everyone will have left here by then, and maybe that is a good idea," I said, thinking it was far too complicated as well as unnecessary, but hoping to make Donna feel better.

"But when you leave here at midnight, you'll be all alone. Can you get someone else to come with you or drop by when you want to leave? Could you ask your friend Stuart to come over and see you out of the building? Or is there anyone else you could ask?"

"There's a Chamber of Commerce meeting tonight and Stuart always goes to that. I don't know how long the socializing part of that event usually lasts since you and I so rarely get there ourselves. So, I certainly couldn't ask him to come with me and just sit and read or something," thinking that I would rather be murdered than ask someone to waste time doing anything so unnecessary. "And I have no idea of how late he stays up;

he might be home in bed asleep at midnight—or eleven o'clock, for all I know. The problem with someone coming by to see me safely out of the parking lot is that if I change my mind—get tired or develop a headache or anything—I'm kind of stuck here instead of being able to leave whenever I want. I really don't think the parking lot is dangerous. It's well-lit and I'll be careful."

"Well you can use your cell phone to keep me posted, and you can call for help if you run into a dangerous situation in the parking lot or anywhere else. Be ready to call me whatever time you leave, no matter how late."

"Now that's a good idea," I said thoughtfully. "If someone jumps out at me brandishing a knife, I can press an automatic dial for 911, and, assuming the call is answered on the first ring, someone can hear me screaming, 'The killer is… gurgle, gurgle… gasp.' I'll use my cell if my car breaks down on the way home. Otherwise, I don't see how it's going to do me much good."

Donna glared at me. We had been watching over each other since we met at the University of British Columbia (UBC) in Vancouver as second-year students. After choosing apartments in the same off-campus student housing project, we became friends, studied together, and shepherded each other through the usual student crises of dropping and adding courses, enduring the stress of exams, falling in and out of love, working part-time jobs, and late night studies and late night parties. At this point in our lives, we had no parents, husbands, siblings, or older relatives watching over us and telling us how to run our lives—just each other, and we never hesitated about giving advice, welcome or not.

"You have to come up with a decent plan for your safety," she insisted. "Both for tonight and Friday. Friday night, phone me when you are ready to leave, and I'll come. I'll line up a babysitter. We'll all watch movies and I'll just come whenever you call. Friday is no problem; tonight is the problem. If you can't come up with a something good, you can't stay. That's all there is to it. The magazine will have to be a little late this month."

"If we lose our deadline at the printer, we'll be more than a little late, and you know what that means," I said, referring to a dark period in our magazine history when a series of disasters caused a chain reaction. We not only missed our printing deadline, we lost our priority at the print shop, and had to wait until two other magazines were printed and the presses were free. Missing our printing deadline meant that we missed a number of advertising deadline offers as well: "Bring in this coupon by blah, blah, blah." Ooops, too late—the coupon deadlines were set two days before our readers received the magazine. The advertisers wouldn't pay us for those ads, of course, and we had to promise them the earth to get them to advertise with us again.

"Think of something," Donna said. "Come up with a plan."

"Actually, I'm pleased and proud to tell you that I have one," I said, rapidly running through some ideas that flashed to mind.

"Oh, yeah? Let's hear it."

"When I come back to the office, I'll bring a thermos of coffee and something to eat so that I won't be calling for food delivery if I find myself getting weak from hunger as the evening wears on. This building is locked up tight at night, and no one can get in without a key because the front and back doors have deadbolt locks. No one would hide in here and wait for everyone to leave in order to corner me tonight because no one knows I am planning to return to work. When I leave at midnight, I'll have my car parked right by the door under the lights in the no parking zone, and there are no bushes nearby and nothing anyone could hide behind. No one will be able to approach me from the rear. Not only that, but to protect myself inside the office, I'll have Raid."

"A raid?" Donna said, puzzled.

"No, I mean Raid." I mimicked holding a spray can aloft and delivered the appropriate sound effects.

"Saints preserve us, what are you talking about?"

"I hate to tell you this, but, to me, the biggest danger tonight is behind the baseboards at the moment. I can't see that our killer has any motive for coming after me, but, in my experience, spiders are indiscriminate in their choice of people they drop on or climb on. I am, therefore, less concerned about meeting a killer in the parking lot than I am about The Thing I might meet locked in this room with me. Bug spray will take care of that."

Donna leaned forward on the desk, her head in her hands, muttering something under her breath that I am happy to report I couldn't hear.

"I'm serious," I said. "I plan to keep the Raid right on my desk so that I'm all ready to defend myself against anything that might decide to come out from behind the baseboard."

Donna raised her head. "I can't believe I went into business with someone like you. What was I thinking? Never mind being armed against a vicious little red spider that might crawl up behind you and scare you, what will happen if a murdering slimeball runs up behind you while you are locking the front door of the building?"

I stared into space for a moment, trying to come up with something more to reduce her anxiety level. "Good point. I'll bring a mirror so that I can see behind me."

"Okay, I'm going to risk being charged with child-neglect just to drive back here at midnight to watch your juggling act. You with your keys, your backpack, and your thermos, holding up a mirror while you lock the front door. I'm bringing my video camera, too. Generations to come should have a chance to enjoy the sight."

"Don't be silly, of course I can do it. I'll bring my thermos and bug spray and the other necessities of life in my backpack. I'll have the mirror in my left hand and the keys in my right to lock the door. If someone comes running, I'll drop the mirror and just step back inside and lock the door. It's a good plan."

Donna shook her head, reached for her purse, and said, "Unless it's Karl, who has a key," but before I could offer a decent protest, she quickly added, "Never mind, I'm leaving while I still have a trace of sanity. When I get home, I'll phone my hairdresser and book a date to color my hair. I can feel the gray looming as we speak."

Since she already colored her hair, I didn't take this announcement too seriously, and merely told her to wish Patrick good luck from me in his game tonight, and that I'd see her at six-fifteen in the parking lot of my apartment building.

I locked up the office at exactly three minutes after five when there were still a comforting number of cars in the parking lot and reached home safely, as I knew I would. I put together a light dinner and brewed strong coffee for my thermos. I stuck a chocolate bar in my backpack in case I started to lose enthusiasm for magazine layout as the night wore on and a sugar rush would be useful. I cracked open a full can of Raid and tested the nozzle out on the balcony to make sure it was operating at peak efficiency. Spiders beware; I was armed and dangerous. I decided not to bother putting a hand mirror in my pack, along with the bug spray and my thermos and bar; I knew I wouldn't use it. I could lock the front door while making a few shoulder checks. A man would have to be an Olympic-class runner to break from around the building or out from the trees without my spotting him in plenty of time to get to safety. I moved my keys onto a key ring that now held only the office key, the key to the front door, and the only key I needed to unlock the car and start the ignition. This would reduce the odds of fumbling for a key I might need in an emergency. After a minute's thought, I dug out the card Mitch had given me with his number and his home phone number scribbled on the back, and tucked it in my pocket. I looked everything over and concluded that I had remembered everything necessary for my comfort and safety and retreated to the balcony.

The sky had clouded over and there were a few drops of rain falling, but I lounged comfortably in my chair, protected by the balcony overhead. I wanted to have a cigarette before the long evening commenced, and I was pleased that I was now down to smoking only one cigarette a day. Maybe I could kick this habit after all, and Donna would never know how long it took me. However, before I could light up, the phone rang, and I decided to run in and answer it in case it was Donna calling to announce that she was going to be late, early, or a no-show for some reason. It was Mandy.

"This will sound peculiar, Sis, but I'm passing on a message from Dodie, my psychic friend. Do you remember her?"

"Yes, of course. What is it?"

"She called me a few minutes ago and said to tell you to be careful around the man in white. It doesn't make much sense but, as usual, she said that it didn't make sense to her either. Do you have any idea what it means?"

"No, I don't," I answered. "I'll have to think about it. I'm also going to go and check my calendar and see if I have a dental check-up scheduled soon. I hope it doesn't refer to my dentist."

"You should assume that it has something to do with all those murders," Mandy spit out, sounding as though she wanted to crawl down the telephone wire and strangle me.

"I'm sorry. I don't mean to sound as though I can't remember the situation here from one day to the next," I said, immediately contrite, "but I hate to have you worry unnecessarily, and I'm not sure how to reassure you that I'm being very careful. I will give Dodie's message serious thought, and if it turns out to be useful advice, I'll be sure and tell you so you can pass the information on to her. And thank her for me. I feel as though the cosmic forces are with me."

"You know, Rachel, it's getting harder and harder for me to figure out when you are kidding and when you aren't. However, I don't have time to worry about it right now. I'm glad you are home from work at a decent hour. I'm on my way out of the shop right now." Her voice lightened. "Josh and I are going to hear a children's folk singer in concert at his school tonight, and he's very excited."

"Wonderful," I exclaimed. "I wish I were going with you. What fun! Tell him I'll be thinking about him."

"I will," said Mandy. "Good night. Love you."

"Love you both," I replied. I hung up the phone and made my way slowly back to the balcony. Never mind how or why Dodie did what she did or even if she did it at all. So many strange things happen in this world that can't be explained, I might as well operate on the premise that this message was critical and correct. Now, where do I go from here?

I sat and smoked my cigarette and tried to apply "man in white" to all the men who were connected to the case. It took me half a cigarette's worth of smoke to come up with the most likely possibility. I looked at my watch and saw that it was almost six o'clock. The question was, would Mrs. T have left her room for dinner by now or not? I stubbed out my cigarette, made the call and just caught her.

Quickly, I ran through a rigmarole invented on the spot as an excuse for phoning and told her I was planning to arrange a photographer to come to The Manor soon, and I'd call a day or two before to make sure she and Seatie were available; I didn't want to interfere with any plans they had; blah, blah, blah; and then got to it.

"In the Navy?" she repeated in answer to my query. "Why, yes, Guy *was* in the navy when he was young."

"Yes, I was talking to him the other day and I believe he said 'Navy.'" I wanted to create the impression we had been chatting about his youth. I raced on, hoping she would forget the question if she reported my call to Seatie or anyone else. "I'm still looking forward to meeting Marianne. I'm sure she will be able to help me with the article. The Manor is such a lovely place to live and I want to do a good job writing about it." I continued to babble with one eye on my watch.

"I guess I should let you go so that you can get to dinner," I said after I had touched on enough subjects for her to lose my question in everything else that I had mentioned. She thanked me very nicely for the call, and it was over. Another piece of the puzzle was in place—perhaps. It was probably Guy and his Navy uniform that she was talking about the other day in reference to Katherine and uniforms. Guy wore Navy whites at one time. Was he the "man in white" who was dangerous to me? However, I mustn't let that influence me too much. Other men wore white, including my dentist, as I had joked to Mandy. My watch now read ten past six and it was time to get down to the parking lot and see if Donna and her two boys had arrived.

-15-

Donna's van was waiting for me at the edge of the parking lot, and after I waved to the family inside, I stopped and put my hands together as though clasping a hockey stick, and faked a shot. I threw my arms overhead, danced around in celebration, and then flashed a thumbs-up sign. My message was unmistakable, and I knew Pat would love it, unlike the man who had just driven into the lot, bringing his car to a halt, riveted, and perhaps debating whether to drive away while he had the chance. I flashed him a reassuring grin, scooted through the light rain and gusty wind to my car, and Donna and I drove in tandem to the Ullman Building.

With dusk approaching and a heavy cloud cover, the lights in the parking lot had already blinked on. The red brick building with its dim nightlights filtering through the windows loomed up from the wet blacktop like a brooding statue emitting an angry glare. For once, I was grateful there were no shrubs or flowers around the characterless entrance so that I was spared the sight of menacing shadows flitting over the face of the building.

As promised, Donna waited as I carefully parked close to the entrance of the building and unlocked the front door. I turned back to flash a smile in the general direction of her van before I entered and locked the door behind me and started up the stairs. The sparsely lit interior was silent, which normally never bothered me, but, tonight, on edge as I was, I found myself breathing hard as I climbed, and was suddenly spooked by the noise when I hit the first squeaky step. I raced the rest of the way up the stairs and didn't calm down until I reached the safety of our office and had locked myself in. I immediately clicked the light switch up and down and up again, went to the front window, and peeked through the venetian blinds. Donna's car turned out of the lot and paused briefly before moving onto the street. They were on their way, and I was alone.

The back office was home territory and comforting, and I pulled out my can of Raid and scanned the walls and floor for the spider. There was no sign of him. Maybe he had fallen asleep behind the baseboard and would stay there all night. I put the can of Raid within arm's reach beside my computer—just in case—and my thermos of coffee and the chocolate bar on Donna's desk. I turned on my computer and was soon engrossed in my work.

About ten o'clock, I leaned back, stretched, and decided it was time for my coffee break. I was munching happily on chocolate between sips of coffee when I heard it. The squeak of the stair outside the door sounded like a bomb blast to my ears. I sat motionless. When the squeak of the second stair sounded, I was on the phone in a flash. With Mitch's card in one hand, I stabbed out his number, and waited tensely for an answer. After four rings, there was a change in tone for the next ring, and knew I would not be speaking to Mitch. The call had been transferred.

As soon as a voice came on the line, I identified myself and said that it was an emergency call from the Ullman Building, and gave the address. "I'm alone in my office on the second floor and someone else is in the building," I said, trying to keep my voice from shaking. "I heard him on the stairs. The cleaning crew comes during the day, and no one but the people in this office use those stairs. There is someone around who shouldn't be in here. Please pass this message on to Inspector Williams or Constable Kerr. Tell them that Guy was once in the Navy, and I need someone here right away. If you can't get a message to them, please send someone else."

I paused, my heart racing, and the voice replied calmly, "I'll take care of it, Ma'am."

I thanked whoever it was, and hung up, suddenly feeling foolish. Why had I said that about Guy? Perhaps it was good that I did. My message might confuse everyone so much, they would come here in a hurry just to find out what I was talking about. Could Karl be on the stairs? He had keys to the front and side doors, but wouldn't he use the side staircase as he always did? I wondered briefly if Karl had ever been in the Navy and then dismissed the idea of foolish Karl being dangerous to anyone but himself. He knew better than anyone about the squeaky stairs and could reach our office by walking down the hall from his own office without my ever hearing him. Besides, if the police weren't satisfied with his alibi but simply didn't have enough evidence to hold him, he would be under surveillance with cops standing by. And why did they have David in custody if they thought Karl was the guilty one?

However, even if the noise turned out to be caused by Karl who had a legitimate reason to be here and had chosen to use the front stairs for some perfectly innocent reason, I decided I was getting the Hell out of Dodge as soon as the police arrived.

I took a deep breath and sat, thinking. With this latest shock came clarity. Who at The Manor was, without question, an "old dude" and would always know when the residents were not in their rooms and could steal their medications very easily? He could slip in and out of the building without being noticed because he looked as old as some of the younger residents and had access to a choice of knives and knew how to use them. And, of course, he wore a white coat at work.

There was a slight sound and I looked up. He was standing in the doorway of the inner office. Somehow, he had opened the locked door without my hearing him.

I eased myself to my feet, taking a very deep breath and letting it out slowly to the count of ten as an icy shock of fear flooded through my body. I might have only one opportunity to save myself and I must be able to move fast at that moment. I was cold and my legs were shaking. I took another deep breath and stood there looking at him. His right arm hung loosely at his side, and in his hand was a knife with a blade that looked shorter than I had imagined. I had one like it in my own kitchen.

He realized I had seen the knife and there was no point in playing games. "You can pick locks," I said, making it a statement.

Jake smiled. "It's always been one of my more useful accomplishments."

I smiled back through stiff lips. "You couldn't have picked the lock on the front door of the building. How did you manage to get in?"

"I had the Renwick woman's key."

His statement barely registered. I concentrated on trying to keep him talking while I calmed myself. "You had everyone fooled."

"A kid waiting on tables yesterday morning heard Mrs. T telling you about my wearing a uniform. I was a courier when I was married to Katherine." Married to Katherine? "Then, today, when I called Johnny, the boy who does the drug pick-up from me, he told me about you. He couldn't give me your name, but I didn't have too much trouble figuring out who it was. I've been watching you from the start. You've been hanging around The Manor and talking to those old biddies. I guessed you were up to something. So, I didn't really fool you, did I?"

"Are you David's father?" I asked, not bothering to hide my surprise at the announcement of his former marriage to Katherine.

"Nah, Katherine married again and had David with her second husband. We were only together for a couple of years when we were young and we got married down East, far away from her mother. Katherine's mother is long dead, the old bat. She never liked me. Katherine has never wanted anyone to hear that she had been married and divorced, not even David. She never told him. Divorce was a bit of a disgrace in the old days, and still is to a lot of people our age, especially to Catholics like us. Things haven't loosened up all that much. Katherine doesn't have any pictures of me; got rid of them all, she said. I doubt if anyone would recognize me even if there were any of me still hanging around.

"Why didn't the marriage last? You are obviously still friends."

"I had a taste for the opposite sex that I couldn't really control."

"She found out that you were being unfaithful?"

"Yeah, but I meant opposite to Katherine's. However, she was always a lady. She understood. I couldn't help myself and she didn't tell anyone. I stayed in touch with her and called her now and then just to see how she was doing. She always had a soft spot for me. She hired me to cook for The Manor when no one else would give me a job. Too old, everyone said, or that's what they thought. But I'm not." And he smiled again and took a step closer.

I moved slightly, too, pressing myself closer to the desk. From the corner of my eye, I could see exactly where the can of Raid was, with its bright orange top. If I made a move toward it, he would guess what I was going to do. I mustn't signal my intent to spray it into his face; he could close his eyes tight enough to be out of danger. Bug spray wasn't mace after all, and I had to get it into his eyes.

"Why did you kill Jody? Did she discover you were stealing drugs from the seniors?"

Jake shrugged. "Maybe not yet, but it was just a matter of time. Jody saw me coming out of old Tibbideau's room during the dinner hour a couple of weeks ago. I hadn't expected anyone to see me, and it kind of caught me by surprise. She asked what I was doing, and I told her that I found his door open, stepped inside to see if something was wrong and realized he had just forgotten to shut it. I had to be especially careful after that. If people started noticing a few of their prescription drugs were missing and complained, Jody might remember my being somewhere that I shouldn't have been; she could have been dangerous to me. Anyway, Katherine wanted her dead, and that helped me decide what to do about my problem."

"What?" I exclaimed, very shocked. "Katherine wanted you to kill Jody?"

"No, of course not, but I know Katherine well. She hated Jody because she thought Jody was after that boy of hers. So, I took care of the problem for her. I owe Katherine a lot."

He shook his head, raised the knife, and ran his thumb along the blade almost absent-mindedly. "Was that stupid or what? Jody had someone else on the string all along. Neither of us knew anything about Karl. I asked Jody to come over here last Monday to price some menu covers for the Halloween dinner and asked her to pick a good picture from whatever the printer had on hand. Told her Katherine approved it. I suggested that she go over to the printer that day during the lunch hour because the printers always take a long time to get stuff like that done, and we didn't have much time.

"She agreed right away. I knew she would. She was well aware that Katherine liked me and wasn't too fond of her. Jody always did what I asked. I had the cap and the clipboard stuck up in a tree and the knife in the ground waiting for me. I had thought of everything I needed and had taken care of it first thing that morning. I understand all about being a courier. No one was going to wonder where that guy was until after I had the job on Jody all wrapped up. It was a good day to kill her; I had lots of time for everything, really."

I pushed this casual attitude to the dispatching of lives from my mind and said, "You took quite a chance coming into this building."

"Nah, I didn't. No one really looks at couriers because there are lots of them, and they're everywhere. If you wear a cap, keep your head down, and carry a clipboard, you can get into almost any building and go anywhere. No one notices you. The real problem was this Karl character. I watched Jody leave The Manor, and she walked around by the road to get here, of course. She always did that; didn't want to get her shoes dirty, I suppose. Or maybe she was afraid of running into a big, bad wolf in the woods."

He laughed briefly. "I took the shortcut through the grounds and walked right through the front door and down the hall. I shut the doors that had been left open so it was kind of dark in that entrance at the side door and waited for her under the stairs. There are never many people in your building. I've been over here a few times. I thought Jody would come past me on her way to the print shop, but she started up the stairs to visit her boyfriend. She must have called and told him she was coming, since the police believe that's why she came over here, and there I was—in the wrong place. I couldn't figure out where she was going, and I had to move fast. But I can move pretty quickly for my age—for any age."

Jake smirked complacently. "It all turned out well. Everything worked out just fine. I walked out the side door when I was finished. I don't think I was gone more than ten or fifteen minutes from The Manor, and the kids on kitchen duty didn't even realize I wasn't there. No one missed me that day. I had a plastic bag to put the knife in after I finished with Jody, and I just took it back with me, washed the knife in my room, and then put it in the dishwasher. I shoved the hat and the clipboard in a couple of different dumpsters a few streets away."

"But Audrey Renwick saw you in this building, and so you had to kill her, too."

"Well, yeah, but I was just making sure. I didn't know if she could have identified me or not. Katherine told me that the printer's assistant—that Audrey person—had seen a Hasty Xpress courier in the Ullman Building right around the time the murder took place and that she might be able to identify him. I hadn't noticed anyone and so I don't understand how the woman could have seen my face, but I couldn't take a chance, of course."

"Well, did she recognize you? Could she have identified you?"

"I have no idea; I never asked her. I never did speak to her. I remembered to take her key to this place, fortunately. Thought it might come in handy, and she had it marked with a piece of tape, and the 'Ullman Building' was written right on it. Glad I had it tonight."

A series of chills ran up and down my spine, and I drew in another deep breath to the count of ten as I braced myself against the edge of the desk to control the shaking of my legs. "Katherine won't be pleased if David continues to be under suspicion for murder. I think she would have preferred to see David married to anyone at all if it was a choice between that and spending his life in prison."

"Yeah, but I didn't know he would come here that day, did I?"

He moved a step closer. I took another deep breath, letting it out slowly, and tensed my muscles to spring.

"It was just bad luck for him. Anyway, I'm going to solve that problem tonight."

"I see," I said, inching my right arm up slightly. Could I risk a quick glance at the can and see which way the nozzle was pointing? No, I couldn't take the chance.

"David is still being held at the police station. You are going to help me clear David right now and then Katherine can relax."

I didn't ask him to explain how I was going to help him. Would the police never get here? Had my message been passed on? My keys were in my purse. How long would bug spray stop him even if I did manage to get it right into his eyes? I could surely outrun him, but where would I be safe? I couldn't unlock my car door and get in and lock the door again before he reached me even if I had my keys, unless there is a secret ingredient in Raid that I haven't heard about. Maybe it would be smart to throw something at him after I sprayed him, or perhaps I should hit him over the head with something. Would I have time? I tried to think of something heavy that was nearby and could do some damage. I didn't want to take my eyes off him.

"Was it you in a black van following me up the Island Highway on the weekend?"

He shrugged. "Part of the way, I guess. I knew you were trouble from the start. Lost you."

There didn't seem to be any point in asking him why he had bothered.

"Did you ever find out why David came over here that day?"

"Nah. It doesn't matter now."

"It was certainly odd," I pressed. "Didn't Katherine tell you why he had come?" I lifted my foot under the right side of the desk and gently began to ease the bottom drawer out. Would there be a telltale squeak? It moved noiselessly outward.

"She didn't know. If David talked much to his mother, she would have realized Jody wasn't interested in him anyway. I don't think they communicate much. I figure he had a little love interest over here himself."

"Really?"

"Probably. He wouldn't say why he was here. So, that would be my guess. Katherine wanted to keep him close to home."

Suddenly, Jake tensed and his eyes narrowed. "What were those old biddies gossiping about when you were talking to them? Mrs. T recognized me, I suppose. Her sister was a friend of Katherine's when they were in school. I've changed my name since then, but I might look familiar to her. She might have figured out who I am."

I had a sudden vision of Mrs. T being attacked by this horrifying man. I must say something to save her in case I wasn't able to escape Jake and his knife.

"We talked about a lot of things," I said. "You just said that a waiter mentioned Mrs. T claimed you used to wear a uniform. She didn't say any such thing. I didn't know about your working as a courier until you told me just now. I guess the waiter didn't realize that she was actually talking about Guy. He used to wear a uniform. He was in the Navy when he was young, Mrs. T told me."

"Ah," said Jake, relaxing. "I guess no one would believe anything she said anyway, so it doesn't really matter. I let it drop to people that she seemed to be pretty senile, and mentioned a few things she'd said or done, all untrue, of course," he admitted, "but she looked at me kind of funny now and then. It was possible that she had recognized me and might tell people that she knew me from the old days. That wouldn't do. Katherine wouldn't have liked that at all. I thought I was going to have to take care of Mrs. T, too. Yeah."

He looked off into the distance smiling faintly as though picturing the elderly woman in her death struggles, and then the smile came off his face as if he suddenly remembered that he didn't have to kill her after all. He took another step forward, and I managed to stop him with another comment.

"I doubt if she realizes who you are. I'm sure she would have been only too happy to identify you as someone she recognized from her youth. You've probably changed a lot since then. Old people love to remember the old days and I'm sure she would have told me about you if she recognized you."

"Yeah, you're right," Jake said, bobbing his head up and down. He didn't place himself in the category of "old people" obviously.

"How did you know I was going to be here tonight?"

"I drove over to your apartment building as soon as I finished cooking dinner. I don't really need to hang around once everything is cooked. I figured I would just check and see how easy it would be to get into your building but, while I was still on the street, out you came. You waved to those people waiting in the van with the motor running, and I saw you clown around a bit. When you got into your car and both of you drove out of the lot, I decided to follow you in case you were coming back here, and that's exactly what you did. I thought the people in the van were going to park in the lot here and wait for you, but they drove off. I assumed you'd decided to work tonight and guessed you were spooked about coming into the building alone. I went back to The Manor and watched TV for a while and then came on over."

I had another question prepared and hurried to get it out before he lost interest in the conversation and came closer. He was already at the front corner of my desk. I assumed he wanted to try to position himself behind me as usual, but I couldn't count on that.

"Aren't you becoming nervous about the number of people you are being forced to kill? Each new death brings the police closer and closer to you. After tonight, they will eliminate David as a suspect. How many more people can you afford to kill before everything points to you and they check out your background?"

Jake actually laughed. "You never heard of a serial killer? They are the hardest to catch, and that's what the cops think this is all about. They don't know what they're doing; they'll never solve this. The killings will stop and they'll be happy and assume whoever it was left town, and it will be someone else's problem. Besides, they wouldn't find anything in my background. I have a different name and a different identity now. Katherine will never tell them anything about me because she will never suspect I was behind any of this. She's easy to fool."

"You certainly planned this well," I said, watching him carefully.

"Yeah, I did. Just one more thing to do."

-16-

When Jake moved, he came at me fast. I stepped up on the edge of the drawer and threw myself across the desk grabbing the Raid as I did so, and had only half rolled onto my back when he was there, leaning over me with his arm up, the lethal blade glinting in the light. I shot the spray into his face and his head jerked back and banged into Cyndi's hanging plant. I had my legs pulled up by then and twisted my body around to bring my legs down on the other side of the desk. There was a frightful racket going on the whole time, which I finally recognized as my own screaming. Jake, blinking his eyes, was staggering around behind the desk.

"Drop the knife!"

Jake and I both froze and looked around, equally startled. My screaming stopped as though a hand had gone over my mouth. Mitch and Bobby were there at last, guns drawn.

Jake blinked rapidly and then looked at the knife he was holding as if surprised to see it in his hand. And then he smiled ingratiatingly at the two officers. "Hello, boys," he said. "I was just showing this little lady the knife I found."

"Drop it," Mitch repeated, and Jake lowered his arm and the knife went clattering to the floor. Bobby moved forward pulling out the handcuffs, and Jake offered no resistance as his arms were pulled behind him and the cuffs snapped onto his wrists.

I was still sitting on the edge of the desk, the can of Raid clutched in my hand, trying to follow what was happening. Mitch stepped towards me, concerned. "Are you all right?" he asked.

"Yes, yes, I'm fine," I said brightly, still not moving from where I sat, legs dangling.

Bobby passed me, pushing Jake ahead of him, and flashed me a dazzling smile. Jake looked over at me, too, still blinking and squinting, and said softly, "No hard feelings, eh? I really had no choice, you know."

I nodded, but couldn't speak. I had the horrible feeling that I might burst into tears any second. I tried a couple of deep breaths and it helped.

Mitch bent over the knife on the floor and was very carefully wrapping it in a white handkerchief before placing it in a bag that he pulled out of his pocket. I wanted to ask him what he would have used to wrap up the evidence if he happened to have blown his nose on his handkerchief, but I thought it might not be tactful. Maybe police officer mucus was factored into any lab analysis. Perhaps I wasn't coping very well now that the danger was all over, and I had better say nothing at all. Everything seemed to be happening in slow motion, and I couldn't stop ridiculous thoughts from running through my mind.

I suddenly caught sight of my red spider slowly spinning its way down from Cyndi's plant, probably disturbed by the bug spray, and I watched as it landed daintily on my desk.

Mitch straightened up and looked at where I was staring. "So, are you going to kill that thing?" he said, looking pointedly at the can of Raid still gripped in my hands. "Would you like me to kill it?"

I shrugged. "I don't care."

He brushed the spider off my desk and it landed on the floor. He hesitated a moment, and then stepped on it. "I have a feeling that if you suddenly decided that you wanted it dead, you might use that spray again and asphyxiate us both," he said. "It's pretty hard to breathe in here as it is."

"You're right," I said, summoning up a smile. "I always did have a heavy hand with the bug spray."

"If you think you can get down off that desk, I'll drive you to the station. We're going to need a statement, and the good news is that you will get a free cup of coffee for all your trouble."

"Okay," I said standing up and happy to find that my legs still worked. "I haven't thanked you yet for coming so quickly. Well, actually, it seemed to take forever, but I guess it wasn't long. Jake arrived about three minutes after I hung up the phone. He picked the lock, and I didn't hear him come in."

"It's a good thing he didn't lock the doors behind him. That would have slowed us up even more. We received your message almost immediately, but we were downtown. It took us a while to cut through the traffic, and we didn't want to use our sirens anywhere near here in case that caused you some trouble. We were having a boring night and were anxious to reach you and hear all about Guy's Navy career."

I laughed, and started for the door, but Mitch put a hand on my shoulder to stop me. "You probably want your backpack, and maybe you don't need that bug spray any longer," he said gently.

I turned around and walked over to my backpack and put the can of Raid inside it. "Yes, I do. This bug spray will have a place of honor in my house, and I'm going to have a special case made to display it. It stopped Jake and I'm not sure how I would have managed without it."

Mitch nodded. "It worked all right."

"I guess you'll be releasing David Parker tonight, won't you?" I said, as we moved towards the door.

"We released him a few hours ago. He's probably at home asleep by now. It seems he has an airtight alibi—he was with his sweetheart Cyndi Wanlass. We couldn't get a straight story out of her because she had 'promised' David she would keep their relationship a secret and she did, even when he was about to be charged with murder and his lawyer told her it was time to break her promise. We had quite a time with her before she realized she had to come clean."

Mitch kept his hand on the small of my back as he opened the front door, followed me out, and waited while I locked it behind us.

"Apparently, David has applied for a job in Vancouver," Mitch continued as we walked down the stairs. The squeaky steps sounded just fine to me when we stepped on them. "Until he is able to leave, he wanted to keep his mother in the dark about what he is doing so that she won't interfere in his love life, which she has done a number of times before. He's learned his lesson."

When we made our way outside, I noticed the parking lot seemed to be filling up with police cruisers—well, a couple of them, at least. I saw two officers hurry over to Bobby and Jake, and I carefully looked away.

"Is that why David was here in the Ullman Building the day Jody was killed? He was coming to see Cyndi?"

"Yes, and she was at his apartment the night Audrey Renwick was killed. He admitted it when we questioned him this time, but we couldn't get confirmation from Cyndi. We wasted a lot of time over that, and I felt like charging her with obstruction of justice or, failing that, with being a half-wit. However, there didn't seem to be much point."

So, they released David a few hours ago, and so he wouldn't have had an alibi if I had been killed. However, David was safe now—and unavailable to Donna as I announced to her when I finally got home and made my call—long after midnight.

Donna was on the phone sounding wide-awake within seconds, no doubt frightened by the late call. As I told my story, she shrieked and exclaimed, "I told you so!" every time I paused to draw a breath, and only calmed down when she discovered both her boys had been woken by the racket she was making and she had to stop and send them back to bed.

"And you're telling me that you took the bug spray not only to use against the red spider but also any killers who happened to be wandering around?" Donna said in a lower tone of voice when she got back on the line. "You really planned for that? How resourceful of you."

"Yes, Raid works well on spiders, but it can slow down a rat, too," I said, "however, I didn't expect anyone to be able to get into the office with the door locked, and I wasn't ready. I had the bug spray on my desk to use against a spider, not a killer. My plan was, once I stepped out of the office, I would have the spray in my hand and my finger on the nozzle and would keep it there as I went down the stairs. Everyone was attacked from behind, remember? I believed the danger zone lay between our office door and the front door, assuming the killer could get in the building. I knew I'd have to do some juggling to open the front door but I would have managed it."

Donna sighed, but "God save us all," was her only comment.

I went on with my story and reached the part where I learned that David and Cyndi were an item, and why David wouldn't tell anyone the reason for his being in the Ullman Building that day. She was as shocked as I had been at first, and made me repeat everything twice, but recovered quickly, and dismissed the Hottie with, "He's happy with Cyndi? Ah well, he's probably a bore, anyway."

"If he is, Cyndi is already working hard to cure him of that bad habit," I said, and we both giggled.

"I'm so glad you called," Donna said. "I wasn't able to sleep wondering if you were still at the office, home in bed, or lying in a ditch somewhere. Thank all the saints in Heaven that it's over, and I think you and I do should do some serious celebrating. You won't have to work tomorrow night and you are finally free to keep any hours you like. Let's go out somewhere and have a great dinner after work. I'll get a sitter."

"Let's do it Saturday night instead," I answered. "I'm already booked for dinner tomorrow night."

"Really? The cop?"

"The cop."

"Well done," Donna said and I could hear the smile in her voice. "Okay, it's time for you to introduce me to your actuary. I'm ready to be reasonable."

"Good," I answered. "And, Donna?"

"Yes?"

"I won't be in to work until about nine-thirty tomorrow morning."

"I figured that," she laughed. "I'll see you when you get there."

We hung up, and I thankfully made my way to bed. I had my life back.

The End

Acknowledgements

Thank you to my children and their spouses who always support my writing, and never fail to ask me how it's going and refrain from rolling their eyes at my long, detailed responses: Berni, who threw me a wild and wonderful launch party for my Viking Mystery Stories for children, and her husband, Michael, who keeps me updated on marketing ideas; Renee, my beta reader, who patiently reads every dreadful draft of all my stories, gives me feedback, and helps name my characters when I am stumped, and her husband, Stephen, who taught me everything I needed to know about being a courier; and Chris, who phones me whenever he has a great idea for a story, which always turns out to be the plot of the latest, most popular movie, and his wife, Sherry, who kept urging me to "write it down" when she found me silently staring into space a number of times during one of my visits, and so I did, and included it as a scene in Murder On A Monday.

Thank you to my high school friends, who have suffered along with me at every stage of my fiction writing: Carolee Fitz-Gerald, Corry-Ann Ardell, and Gayle Jackson, writers all; and to Marianne Fourt, who drove me around Nanaimo to refresh my memory of the town I hadn't seen for years, and to my sister-in-law, Marilyn Grenier, who helped select the most likely building in Victoria for the home of my heroine, Rachel. Thank you to Della Connor for her ongoing encouragement and marketing help, Doug Milne, who introduced me to his writers' club, and Doug Hay, who arranged the design of my website and taught me the ins and outs of social media marketing.

Thank you to High Tide Publications Incorporated and the kind staff for selecting my book to publish when they are inundated with so many queries and choices, and to Narielle Living, my editor, for her help and her positive outlook.

And to everyone who ever said anything even vaguely positive to me about my writing—I heard you and I thank you.

About the Author

Maureen Grenier has loved mystery stories since she was a child—reading, writing, watching, and listening to them. She was born and raised in British Columbia and lived for a while in Victoria. She moved to Ontario, raised three children, taught school, was an artist for *The Kanata Standard*, an editor and writer for *Meridian Magazine*, and Publications Manager for the Canadian Institute of Actuaries. Maureen is an elementary school teacher (U of Victoria), trained as a commercial artist (Washington State U), and has a BA from the U of Waterloo. She is now living in BC as a freelance editor and writer and has published two sports mysteries for children, and is putting the final touches to her second Rachel Mathews mystery, *Murder On A Tuesday*.

Other Books by Maureen Grenier

Maureen has written and illustrated two Viking Club Mysteries for children ages 8-12:
- *Something's Missing*, published in 2012 – a hockey sports-mystery
- *Someone's Trapped*, published in 2014 – a soccer sports-mystery

Watch for the next Rachel Mathews Murder Mystery, *Murder On A Tuesday*, coming soon!